"We...

Amy ...

"I'll send our pilot to ...
in Las Vegas by midnight."

Amy leaned against the doorjamb, watching him and wondering whether she should laugh or call the loony bin patrol.

"Well, what do you think? Will you marry me?" Max asked tenderly, his hand slipping onto her shoulder to pull her closer.

She made the mistake of glancing into those blue eyes. *Yes*, a breathless voice almost agreed.

Then Amy caught herself. Two days ago Max was waiting to wed Robin. Amy didn't want a rebound husband. And even if that stumbling block didn't exist, their brief acquaintance hardly measured up as friendship, much less marriage.

Amy crossed her arms defensively. "It boggles my mind we're having this discussion. I know you're joking, but it isn't funny."

"Some things I don't joke about. Proposing marriage is one of those things. Marry me, Amy."

ROMANCE

Dear Reader,

A wedding at historic Durham House Bed and Breakfast in Houston, Texas, sparked the idea for *The Wedding Escapade*.

Although picture-perfect ceremonies are the wish of every bride and groom, inevitably something goes awry—something minor like rings misplaced, something major like cakes dropped or the officiant not showing up. Tears are shed, hands are wrung, then the mishaps become part of family lore.

Weddings and wedding glitches just naturally cause a romance writer's imagination to take flight. For example—Amy, a bridal consultant, her career dependent on successful ceremonies, and one of her high-profile weddings self-destructs at the last minute, leaving the groom on her hands....

Harlequin Romance was celebrating its thirtieth anniversary when the first Kate Denton book was released. Back then, writing was part-time, squeezed in on nights and weekends. Now it's become a full-time career and a fulfilled dream of storytelling for the Harlequin Romance audience.

A toast to Harlequin Romance and its fortieth anniversary...a successful collaboration of publisher, editors, writers and, most important, you, the readers.

Kate Denton

The Wedding
Escapade
Kate Denton

Harlequin Books

TORONTO • NEW YORK • LONDON
AMSTERDAM • PARIS • SYDNEY • HAMBURG
STOCKHOLM • ATHENS • TOKYO • MILAN
MADRID • WARSAW • BUDAPEST • AUCKLAND

To Marguerite Swanson, for her friendship, her hospitality at Durham House Bed and Breakfast, and—most of all—for sharing her love and knowledge of the Houston Heights.

ISBN 0-373-03452-0

THE WEDDING ESCAPADE

First North American Publication 1997.

CHAPTER ONE

"WELL, if all else fails, we can bring in the UN to mediate." Amy added a chuckle to blunt the barb, but the sardonic smile she received from Max Evans told her the message had been duly noted.

"Cute," he remarked.

Amy opened her mouth for a second volley, then closed it. Despite her exasperation, and despite the fact Max Evans wasn't exactly a male version of Miss Manners, sniping at clients was ill-advised. Pity. Oh, how she'd love telling him how she felt about his boorish behavior. The man apparently thought a matinee-idol face and Roman-god physique gave him latitude to act as he pleased. Not in Amy Holt's book it didn't.

In truth, she wasn't sure who annoyed her more—Max or his whiny fiancée, Robin Porter. But she *was* sure the couple seated across from her at the lace-clothed table were driving her to distraction.

Without a doubt, these two deserved each other. *May this union become their own private purgatory*, she implored, eyes heavenward, as Max and Robin launched back into their heated argument over the number of wedding guests and attendants. It was Amy's third meeting with the pair and the previous sessions had been every bit as frustrating and fractious.

Unused to such indecorous conduct, Amy's irritation soared. Never before had she harbored a desire such as this one—to be a burly bar bouncer and eject these clients from the premises by the seats of their couturier pants.

"Remember...my home can only hold a hundred people," she said, taking a deep breath before interrupting the latest exchange. "Are you positive you want to be married here?" It wasn't the first time she'd posed the question. The bride-to-be clearly envisioned an affair more elaborate than Torrence Place could accommodate. "Perhaps a church or a country club where numbers are not a problem." *Perhaps the Astrodome or Rice Stadium.* "I've—"

"Do you mind?" Max Evans cast a reproachful scowl in her direction. "I'm having enough trouble getting through to Robin without having to fight you, too."

If a banana cream pie had been handy, Amy would gladly have thrown it in his arrogant face. And to think how awestruck she'd been with him initially, even going so far as lamenting how "the good ones are always taken."

That earlier image of Max Evans was branded in Amy's memory. He'd been heart-stoppingly handsome in a dark custom-tailored suit, crisp white shirt and blue designer tie, selected no doubt to flatter his long-lashed, blue-violet eyes and curly black hair. The effect—dazzling then—was wasted on her now. Exposure to dose after dose of his domineering ways made Max's looks about as relevant as lips on a snake. Nothing less than a lobotomy could draw Amy to this man again.

But like it or not, she had to put up with him. So she sat there, twisting a strand of strawberry-blond hair and quietly stewing, all the while wondering if the future held many more scenarios like this one. If so, she might come to seriously question her career choice.

Since childhood, Amy had cherished everything about weddings—the spectacle, the music, the drama of a man and woman pledging eternal devotion. That's why she'd become a wedding consultant. From the pomp of cathedral events with a host of bridesmaids and an audience of a thousand to the intimacy of cozy affairs with a dozen guests—Amy loved it all. *Until this particular bride and groom happened along.*

"A hundred's the limit. And one attendant each. *One*, Robin." Max Evans's raised voice reclaimed Amy's attention. "I'm not budging on this. I've told you all along I want a simple service."

"But, darling..." Robin fiddled with her engagement ring—a setting of diamonds and sapphires Amy considered too large and too flashy for comfort or taste—and fluttered her eyelashes at him.

"No 'but darlings,'" he chided, refusing to yield to the eyelashes.

Robin's lips formed a pout. "I didn't know you meant *this* simple. It's bad enough we're putting it together in such a rush. Who knows what everyone will think? Then to have a bare-bones ceremony, too. We might as well get married by a justice of the peace if you're going to limit everything."

"A J.P. sounds great about now."

"Ohhh, Max," Robin wailed. "If you keep talking like that, I just may back out all together."

Vexation rising, Max agitatedly jiggled his foot. Why couldn't Robin understand his desire for a "plain vanilla" wedding? She'd seemed to at first. But now, now she acted more enamored of the process itself than of marrying him. Like all that mattered was putting on the grandest show possible. The comments of this highly recommended wedding planner were definitely not helping. Amy Holt was all too happy aiding and abetting Robin in her excesses.

"I've tried to address your wishes, Robin," he said through gritted teeth. "You're the one wanting a long honeymoon in Hawaii. And you're the one whose as-

trologer picked Thursday as 'consistent with your sign.'"
At that Max rolled his eyes. "My calendar's not that
flexible. It's stay with this date or—"

"Okay, okay!"

Amy's gaze widened at this rare flash of temper from
the young woman. She turned to Max, who appeared
unruffled by the outburst.

"All right, that's settled," he announced. "What's
next?"

Not much, Amy thought wryly, only the flowers,
cakes, food, drink...myriad details. A dull headache
began forming in her right temple. As if their being late
this morning wasn't inconvenience enough, Max and
Robin had already been here an hour and all that had
been resolved was the number of guests and size of the
wedding party.

Obviously, the fact that she might have other respon-
sibilities did not concern them. Three more appoint-
ments awaited her today and from the looks of things,
she'd be racing around playing catch-up the entire
afternoon.

"The officiant?" she suggested, discreetly checking
her watch and hoping she'd picked a topic the two
wouldn't argue about.

"Reverend Hulse," Max answered without a glance
Robin's way. "He's an old family friend."

The young woman nodded in benign agreement.
Wimp. If Amy were the bride, she'd have told Max to
take a hike, and to take Reverend Hulse with him.

The lifting of her hand for a quick kiss, like the one
he was bestowing on Robin, wouldn't have swayed her,
either—although it worked on Robin, who smiled at the
gesture. No wonder he kept getting his way; he was
manipulative as well as stubborn. He was also exceed-
ingly rich.

If Max's elegant handsomeness wasn't sufficient to hold a fiancée, there was that added lure of Evans dollars, millions of them. Originating with the Texas requisites of oil and cattle, the family fortune had evolved into a revenue-generating machine, with Max's share as one of the biggest cogs. He had parlayed his own sizable endowment into greater riches through savvy real estate transactions, a Greenway Plaza high rise bearing the Evans name attesting to his many profitable ventures.

Commercial property development was Max's specialty and he'd been skillful in attracting several large corporations to Harris County and the surrounding southeast Texas area. Amy didn't know much about real estate dealings, but the newspaper and television often mentioned Max's solid gold instincts.

So, maybe that devastating combination of affluence and looks caused Robin to overlook his intimidating ways. Maybe she even rationalized that a major coup like snaring Max Evans from the bachelor ranks compensated for a probable future of total domination. Undoubtedly, her friends were envious and her family overjoyed that she'd made such a splendid match.

Amy was not impressed. She longed to fling the man's deposit back at him with instructions on just where to put it. Unfortunately, she didn't have the luxury of telling him off. His was the fattest fee she'd ever received for a wedding and she desperately needed the cash. A humongous plumbing bill had arrived in the morning mail, then there was— *Take it easy*, she scolded. *Now isn't the time to worry about that. Not while you still have these two on your hands*.

As she strove for inner calm, Amy concentrated on the benefits this wedding would bring her and her company. So the prospective bride was a sniveler and the groom terminally obnoxious. Nevertheless, the marriage would receive abundant media coverage, free advertising to generate new clients.

Both families were wealthy and prominent and each had long-standing memberships in the Texas aristocracy, including two former governors and roots dating back to the Texas Revolution. Yes, the press interest would be high. *If only the two weren't such royal pains.*

"Next item?"

Max's question interrupted Amy's musings. She looked down at the notes in her lap. "The actual ceremony will be held in the gazebo...right?"

Surprisingly, both Max and Robin nodded in agreement. "You will, of course, be prepared to shift everything inside in the event of rain?" he asked.

"Of course," Amy echoed, plastering a false smile on her face. What did he want—a blood oath? She'd already assured him that contingency plans were in place. The outdoor ceremony was scheduled for mid-April—a mere three weeks from today—and spring weather was unpredictable in Houston. But that was beside the point. *As if I have to be told how to do my job,* Amy thought, her sensibilities continuing to rankle. While Max Evans might know everything there was to know about making money, he was no expert on weddings. From all she'd heard, he'd spent the better part of his life avoiding them.

"Why don't we move on to the food and drink, and after that, the flowers?" Amy said, affecting a pleasant tone.

Max's watch beeped and he glanced down at the dial. "'Fraid we'll have to table that for now. I have a meeting at the Petroleum Club in twenty minutes. We'll call you to set up another get-together." He stood, holding his hand out to Robin to assist her from her chair. Within seconds, they were gone.

Amy lingered at her front door watching them drive off in Max's silver Lexus coupe and wondering if the three of them could come to terms before the day of reckoning. She could envision the wrangling still going on as the processional began.

Maybe she should insert a clause in future contracts restricting the number of planning sessions. She couldn't afford to have multiple meetings on every point. But in this case, she reminded herself, she couldn't afford not to. No matter how disagreeable these clients, there were generous profits to be banked. Profits she needed. The wolves weren't just at the door—they were already inside the house, nipping at her heels.

Speaking of wolves nipping... She dashed to the study for her purse and car keys. She was overdue for a meeting with her banker to talk about a loan for phase two of the upstairs renovations.

It was after seven when Amy drove home down Heights Boulevard to Torrence Place. The walkers and joggers on the grassy esplanade that divided the boulevard gave a semblance of normalcy to what had been a truly demanding day, emotionally and physically. First Max and Robin, then the loan officer advising her it would be unwise to invest any more capital until her business "matured"—whatever that meant, then scrambling to make a bridal fashion show at a northside mall, and zigzagging through the rush-hour traffic to attend an open house at a new restaurant courting reception business.

She discarded her suit jacket and kicked off her shoes with a grateful "aah" the minute she got in the rear door. The tail of her silk blouse had already been freed from her skirt and the buttons undone when the doorbell rang. "What now?" she groaned, hastily trying to put herself back together.

Max could see her shadowy approach through the leaded-glass door panel. He'd sooner be sitting in his dentist's chair undergoing a root canal, as be here on Amy Holt's porch preparing to eat crow. But he had no choice. He'd acted abominably this morning, subjecting the wedding consultant to his rotten humor. So Robin was grating on him lately. That was nobody's fault but his own . . . certainly not Amy Holt's.

Max wasn't the only one dreading this encounter. As soon as she saw who it was, Amy wished she'd remained in the rear, pretending not to be home.

His eyes slowly took her in, the stockinged feet, blouse hanging over her skirt, then he smiled, making Amy all too aware of her disheveled state. "Sorry to barge in," he said, handing her a huge bouquet of pink tulips. "But I wanted to bring a peace offering. I've worried all day about how discourteous Robin and I were to you this morning, being late, then involving you in our petty squabbles. My apologies."

Amy hesitantly acknowledged the flowers. "I'm used to . . . nerves," she said, the pause giving away the fact that she believed his having an attack of pre-wedding nerves was about as likely as his fretting over what had transpired today. *At least he's attempting to make amends.*

"Please don't give it another thought," she added graciously, stroking one of the tulip petals.

"Then we're all squared away?"

"Of course."

For an instant he stood there looking as if he wanted to say more, but instead he mumbled "Great" before turning and trotting back down the steps. He was almost to the curb when Amy shut the door.

*   *   *

"The flowers are lovely," Stephanie told her, eyeing the tulips in the hall. "But it's time a man was bringing you flowers, instead of your buying them yourself."

Amy didn't respond. For some reason, she didn't care to admit that a man *had* brought them. Least of all this man. Maybe she feared revealing to Steph how ridiculously pleased she was by Max's gift.

"So how are those favorite clients of yours?"

There was no need for Stephanie to identify "those clients." Amy had rambled on for hours about the discordant sessions with Max and Robin. But it struck her as uncanny that Steph should bring them up at this particular moment. Had she spotted Max here the other night? It would have been easy for her to do so.

After acquiring Torrence Place, Amy had sought renters for the adjacent carriage house. Stephanie Anders, a private-duty nurse, and her husband Jay, a medical resident, had applied. Like Amy, they loved the Heights neighborhood and wanted to live there. When Stephanie sweetened the deal with an offer to work part-time in Amy's wedding business, Amy saw it as the perfect solution to her personnel needs. She couldn't afford a regular assistant's salary and Stephanie could shuffle her hospital hours to accommodate Amy's schedule.

Within weeks, the neighbor-employee relationship had blossomed into friendship. The close association also meant Stephanie was privy to most of the comings and goings at Torrence Place.

But knowing Steph as she now did, Amy also knew that she hadn't glimpsed Max. Stephanie had no flair for subtlety. If she'd spied him alone and bearing flowers, Steph would already have subjected Amy to a grilling worthy of the fiercest litigator.

"They get more combative every time I see them," Amy said. Having determined Stephanie's inquiry to be innocent, Amy relaxed and filled her in on the couple's most recent visit. "And if that wasn't enough, Robin called me yesterday with extra demands." Amy grabbed a saucepan from the overhead rack.

Stephanie was standing at the kitchen island, icing a two-tiered wedding cake. "Then Robin was the one who added the caged doves and the strolling violinists to the 'To Do' list?"

"Yes, and the pâté swan and monogrammed ice sculpture. I'm amazed a skywriter and some strutting peacocks weren't included. When it comes to special effects, Robin could probably orchestrate the opening ceremonies of the Olympics." Amy dumped water and a dollop of butter into the pan and turned on the burner.

"But I thought Max wanted something understated and tasteful. How did she get him to go along with these showy extras?"

Amy shrugged. "I have no idea. She's his fiancée and—" The ringing doorbell stopped her. "One moment," she called out. "Steph, can you take over these Grand Marnier puffs for me?" The bell rang again.

"I'm coming, I'm coming," Amy grumbled under her breath, grabbing a tea towel to wipe her hands as she went to answer the door.

Spying him through the glass, she gave a groan similar to two nights ago. *Speak of the devil—Max Evans again*. And looking none too happy, she thought as she opened the door to a cloudy face overshadowing a vibrant yellow polo shirt. Obviously, this particular groom wasn't on Amy's front porch early on a Saturday to exchange pleasantries.

Why now of all times, Amy moaned, when she was too consumed with work to indulge him? Experience provided her an immediate answer. She'd been around long enough to know and accept the fact that clients didn't always choose convenient moments, especially wealthy clients. People like Max were accustomed to deference at every turn. She might as well listen to his concerns and get it over with. "Oh, hello," she said. "I didn't expect to see you this morning. Tell me how I can help you, Mr. Evans."

"I thought *hiring you* would help me," he griped. "I believed we had an agreement on the kind of wedding you were to put on. That's why I chose Torrence Place. Now I find you're turning it into a three-ring circus." He braced one hand on the door frame and leaned intimidatingly in her direction.

"Now, just a darned minute..." Amy, momentarily losing her cool, glared up at him from her diminutive height, her brown eyes shooting sparks. Influential client or not, she wasn't about to put up with being blamed for something not her fault. "I wasn't hired to countermand your intended. The choices are hers, not mine."

"With your encouragement, according to Robin. I've already paid for the wedding I wanted. I suggest you quit trying to run up the tab with a bunch of extras."

"*My* encouragement? *Me* run up the tab? I'll have you know—"

"And *I'll* have you know that I don't intend to put up with this...this folderol. Small and simple. Surely that was clear. It shouldn't take a rocket scientist to figure out why I spent so much time personally overseeing the decisions."

"Tell that to—" Amy paused, forcing down her temper. She had nothing to gain by maligning his bride-to-be and making him madder than he already was. "Why don't we continue this conversation inside?" She could just imagine the reactions of neighbors or passersby witnessing her in a heated confrontation on the front porch.

"What I have to say won't take much longer."

"Be that as it may, I'm cooking, and what I have on the stove can't wait," Amy answered. "If you want to talk to me right now, it'll have to be in my kitchen." She led Max to the rear of the house, introduced him to Stephanie and gestured toward a chair. Max ignored the chair. Instead he hovered over Amy at the stove as she took the wooden spoon from Stephanie and began stirring the puff mixture.

"Now about your wedding," Amy said, trying to maintain a modicum of composure. He was too close for comfort. She could detect a hint of spicy after-shave and feel the fabric of his cotton knit shirt against her arm. "Am I to make changes to your *fiancée's* selections?" Amy hoped he caught the emphasis. She was doing her best to be civil, but Max Evans must realize that she was through being bullied. "I'd appreciate knowing as soon as possible, before I go 'running up the tab' any more."

"Forget I said that. Naturally I'll reimburse you for any additional costs. I just hope importing the Vienna Boys' Choir is not on the agenda."

"Oh, nothing that ostentatious...yet." She beat the batter in the saucepan furiously.

"Would you care for coffee?" Stephanie interjected, apparently discerning that a peacemaker was needed.

To Amy's astonishment, Max agreed. He sat down at the kitchen table, sipping a cup of mocha java and chatting amicably with Stephanie while Amy dropped teaspoonfuls of the batter onto baking sheets. With the puffs in the ovens, she poured a cup of coffee for herself and joined them at the table.

"Now let's clarify what I'm supposed to do," she said. "In the next few weeks, do I get approval from you on every detail?"

"Surely you can sort out when I need to be contacted."

"Even if that were true, I shouldn't have to. My job is consultant, not referee."

He pulled out a checkbook and pen and scribbled another payment. "That should provide for any other exigencies, including 'refereeing,' as you put it." He tossed the check on the table.

Amy fixed her gaze on the figures for an instant, eyes almost popping at the total. It took all her resolve not to grab the check and kiss it. Reluctantly, she tore it in two and slid the pieces in his direction. Just because the amount was a mere pittance to Max, didn't mean she could take advantage of him. So far his initial fee had sufficiently covered all costs, with room left for a tidy profit. "I wasn't asking for more money—just a little consideration." There was no missing the bite to her words.

The nasty retort she expected from him did not materialize. Instead Max looked somewhat taken aback as he picked up the two pieces of check and put them in his pocket. "Most people I know would love getting more money."

"I'm not most people."

A corner of his mouth twitched in a betraying smile. "I'm beginning to appreciate that. I meant no offense."

Again, Amy was caught off guard. She didn't know what to make of Max. Sometimes—like now—he was almost human, the dictatorial pose completely gone.

He stood up. "I'll talk to Robin. From here on you'll consult with me and only me. Got it?"

The dictator was back. "Yes, sir." Amy rose and clicked her heels together.

"Thanks for the coffee," he said politely to Stephanie, then without further conversation, or even a goodbye to Amy, he turned and left.

Amy followed after him to the front door, once again watching as he drove off. When she reappeared in the kitchen, Stephanie had removed the puffs from the oven and returned to the cake icing.

"Thank goodness he's gone." Amy slumped down into a nearby chair and exhaled loudly. "So what did you think?"

"Who can think? What a gorgeous hunk of man."

"With the disposition of a drill sergeant."

"Oh, he's just frustrated…probably with good reason, from what you've been telling me about Robin. Anyway, we'll both be laughing about all this once the wedding's over."

Amy raised an eyebrow. "Are you sure of that?"

"Positive. Meanwhile, whenever the pressure starts getting to you, just picture all the new commissions you'll attract because of those two. Torrence Place and 'Arrangements by Amy' will be on the lips of the best people. More jobs, bigger bucks. One of these days you'll end up the richest old maid in Houston."

"Please." Amy gave Stephanie an entreating frown. "You're not going to lecture me on that again, are you?"

Stephanie pointed a spatula at Amy. "Somebody has to. The only socializing you do involves other people's lives—not yours."

"So?" Amy rose to load the dishwasher. "Quit fretting, Steph. I'll find myself a nice guy one of these days."

"How many days do you intend to wait? You're already twenty-nine and, by your own admission, have never been serious about anyone." Stephanie brightened. "Here's an idea—why don't you steal Mr. Gorgeous from the 'bird lady'?"

"Now that would be a smart move." Amy gave Stephanie an incredulous shake of the head. "Not only would my name be mud after Robin's family finished with me, but the man is impossible."

"He didn't seem all that bad."

"He was on his good behavior, Steph. You haven't seen him at his worst."

"Maybe it's Robin. Maybe she brings out the beast in him. Could be he just needs 'luv' from the right woman."

Amy let out an exaggerated sigh. "Stephanie Anders, you're hopeless. Whether she's 'right' or not, he's already got a woman and you and I have a wedding to put on tonight. Now let's hustle. The helpers will be here soon to set up."

After the last glass had been washed and shelved and the house restored to normal that evening, Amy headed for her bedroom. It was almost one a.m. and she was exhausted. All she could do was slip into her nightshirt, quickly brush her teeth, then collapse into bed.

She had anticipated that sleep would claim her immediately, but instead, she lay awake thinking about Max and Robin. Something set them apart from most of the couples she'd worked with. Not the bickering. Pre-wedding jitters could explain that away. No, there just seemed to be an element missing in their relationship. These two lacked that special spark so evident with other brides and grooms. Intuition told Amy it wasn't a good match and the possibility sent a wave of depression washing over her. She had a foreboding about their future, and about her role in it.

Cool it, Miss High and Mighty, she cautioned herself. Your job is to orchestrate the wedding, not assume responsibility for the happily-ever-after. She thought about Stephanie's suggestion that Amy steal Max for her own. Leave it to Stephanie to come up with such a capricious notion.

Amy flipped onto her stomach and tried to fall asleep, but to no avail. She could forget Robin, but couldn't banish Max from her mind. He was different from most of the first-time grooms. Older, for one thing. Amy knew from the many articles in the Houston newspapers that Max was in his late thirties, not exactly boyish.

For years Max Evans had been one of the most written-about bachelors in Texas. Among others, he'd squired movie stars, a former Miss Texas, a TV anchorwoman and a member of the British royal family. There had been many a broken heart left in his wake, but, interestingly, no bitter backstabbing from any of those old flames.

So why after all this time and all those women was he committing to someone like Robin Porter, when he could have almost anyone he set his sights on? It didn't add up.

What would it be like to have been one of those women? To kiss him? Amy punched her pillow, trying to get comfortable and to will away such inappropriate thoughts. Darn that Stephanie. Her outlandish suggestion had caused this flight of fancy. Max was off-limits. Not only was he a business contact, but an engaged contact at that and, as such, totally beyond her grasp. Amy was worn-out, but now she was almost afraid to fall asleep. The way her mind was deteriorating, she'd probably dream about Max.

CHAPTER TWO

APPARENTLY Max Evans had issued a firm edict to his bride-to-be, because Amy received no more contacts from Robin. He, however, phoned daily to monitor her activities, a practice which grated on Amy's already-raw nerves. Max and Robin's accelerated wedding date had her working against the clock and she simply couldn't tolerate more demands.

When Max made a third drop-in visit the next Thursday, Amy was ready to throw in the towel and cry "enough!"

"I see everything's progressing as planned. This arrived at my parents' house yesterday." He stood on the front step, brandishing one of the thick vellum invitations in his hand.

Amy found his actions offensive, as if he were astounded that she *was* on schedule. Max Evans had no reason for doubting her ability to get things done and it was time to put him in his place. "Am I the exception or do you micro-manage every one of your business transactions? Is it common practice to peek over the shoulder of the property appraisers, double-check the accountant's figures and proofread your secretary's letters?"

Max ruffled his forehead. "Sorry. I didn't realize that's what I was doing. From all appearances the preparation is running along quite smoothly."

She was not placated. *Smoothly, my foot. If he only knew half of what it took to achieve that impression.* Most weddings required a full year of preparation—six

21

months at a minimum. The few weeks she'd been given for this one was a major push.

But no use complaining to him of the brouhaha at the printer's brought about by the rushed-up invitations, or mentioning the untold hours spent addressing each envelope in ornate calligraphy. Amy could go on and on. But to what purpose? Max hadn't coerced her into taking the job. She'd accepted it willingly. And pressing the point wouldn't generate any sympathy, probably just cause another check to be thrown her way.

Rather than inviting him in, Amy stepped outside and closed the door behind her. No matter what the provocation, she would maintain her equilibrium. It was a lovely April afternoon, the sky a flawless blue, the temperature near perfect. Amy had no wish to ruin her day with a tedious Max Evans confrontation.

She wondered why he'd really come by. Surely one of his pesky phone calls could have sufficed to acknowledge that the invitations were being received.

Max walked over to the porch swing, unbuttoned his suit coat and sat down, a shove of his foot sending the swing in motion. It appeared that Mr. Evans intended to stay and chat awhile, a notion which piqued Amy's interest even further.

She eased onto the porch railing and leaned against a supporting post. While waiting for Max to make the first move, she focused her attention to the street. A young family was peddling by on a bicycle built for two—converted now to three, with the addition of a baby seat for their chubby toddler. Could she visualize Max and Robin in this picture of domestic bliss? Not a chance. It was difficult enough to see them as a happy couple, much less as a devoted trio.

"By the way, have you heard from Robin?" he finally said.

So that's the real purpose of your visit. "No, should I have?"

"Not necessarily."

"Then why are you asking?" *And asking me instead of her*? "Also, why did you make a personal trip to do so?"

"Maybe it just gave me an excuse to see you." He casually framed the swing back with his arms as he maintained its motion.

Amy tried to stifle the ridiculous surge of pleasure rising from his words, despising herself for feeling as she did. She wasn't in the habit of coveting other women's fiancés, and she couldn't afford to start now—especially not with this man, who was all too capable of punching her buttons. Good thing he was such an irritant or she might need that lobotomy after all to avoid falling for those engaging blue eyes and that enigmatic grin...

"Does Robin know you're toying with the hired help?" Amy's voice was deliberately tart. She had to remind Max, as well as herself, of their positions. After all, he was going to be married in two weeks. And she'd been retained to ensure that the nuptials came off without a snag.

He smiled. "Don't trouble yourself about Robin. She's not the jealous kind. Even with 'hired help' as beautiful as you."

Amy worked at hiding a blush. Despite the pleasant morning, suddenly she felt transported to Houston in midsummer, when the heat and humidity turned the city into nature's own sauna. Her cotton shirt was beginning to stick to her skin and her hair felt hot on the back of her neck.

It was difficult not to be taken in by the compliment, even though it was likely as hollow as the statement that Robin wasn't the jealous type. Having met the young woman, Amy knew Max's assessment was inaccurate. Robin had clung to her guy like plastic wrap and emitted "he's taken" signals to Amy whenever the three of them had been together.

Of course, in this instance, Amy could hardly blame Robin. Max might be a groom pushing forty, but the tiny creases at the corners of his eyes and few strands of silver at his temples only made him more handsome, maybe too handsome for his own good. He was charming, to boot, when he put his mind to it. Like today as compliments rolled effortlessly off his tongue and kept her off balance. "Uh…do you need anything else…?" Amy stammered.

The blush could no longer be suppressed once she caught the glint in those intriguing eyes of his. Max knew he was disconcerting her and he was reveling in it. Did Robin know what she was letting herself in for? Max would manipulate her shamelessly, and a smile from him would have her begging for more.

Robin Porter might be a major nuisance but right now she had Amy's sympathy. Amy stood up. The flashback to Max's fiancée had provided the impetus she needed for ending this fruitless conversation. "If we have no other business, then I trust you'll excuse me," she said formally. "I have an engagement across town."

Max stood, also, pulling at the French cuffs of his shirt and straightening his onyx links. He retrieved a business card from his suit pocket along with a pen to scribble on the reverse side. "This is my secretary's name and number in case I'm out of touch. She'll know where to reach me. Now I'd better let you get to that…engagement." He tipped his hand in an informal salute and left.

*   *   *

The information about Max's secretary was superfluous since he continued to call Amy every day. At first, the conversations had been short and to the point, centering solely on details of the upcoming rites. Now they were talking longer and more personally, straying to such disparate subjects as movies, a recent exhibition at the Contemporary Arts Museum, an upcoming pop concert at Jones Hall, even the Astros or Rockets sports teams.

Then as if to demonstrate that Robin was not forgotten, and that the call was in fact business-based, Max closed each discussion on a note related to his wedding. Like a chameleon changing its colors, he then switched from friendly banterer to pompous inquisitor, managing to antagonize Amy in the process. The worst part was that no matter how aggravating the end of the previous call, she'd actually be looking forward to the next one.

"I must be losing it," she muttered aloud. "Feeding on a relationship that doesn't even exist and simpering like a teenager over a man I don't approve of." Maybe the pressure was getting to her. Or maybe the lack of an adequate social life of her own was causing her to react to Max this way. She gave a sigh of relief when, on Wednesday, Max told her he was leaving town, reiterated his secretary's number, and said that he'd check with Amy when he returned.

Considering his pattern of late, she'd expected to hear from him anyway, but there was no word until Saturday, when he once more appeared on her doorstep. *We have to quit meeting like this*, Amy started to say when she answered the bell.

"I've been in Denver," he said as if feeling the need to explain. "Just got in this morning."

It must have been a demanding trip, because he looked tired, the lines around his eyes more pronounced than usual, a touch of weariness in his face. Probably working too hard to get business out of the way before the honeymoon, she surmised. Amy shook her head; she was *definitely* losing it if she'd begun to fret about Max's health.

"Miss me?" he asked, not so tired that he couldn't still be flip.

"Hardly," she lied, realizing she'd done just that, her attraction seeming to have grown even stronger during her brief vacation from his meddling. "I've been too busy with wedding details to give the individual participants much thought." *There, that should put him in his place*, even if the declaration was a blatant distortion of the truth. She'd thought about him, fantasized about him, and just as she once feared, dreamed about him.

"Got any of that good coffee? I could use a cup." Warily, Amy invited him inside and led the way to her kitchen. While Max had been away she'd resolutely concentrated on every fault she could attribute to him, and in mantra fashion recited those failings frequently. The way he was overbearing, always determined to have the upper hand . . . his arrogant attitude and unorthodox approach to marriage.

Amy had begun to deduce from his behavior that Max didn't love Robin—not by Amy's definition of love. He was marrying for convenience, she suspected. There was simply no other explanation. One more blot on his character as far as she was concerned. Not that the blot was having much effect on her at the moment as she daydreamed about caressing away those worry lines on his forehead.

Straightening her back, Amy again resolved to remember how lucky she was *not* to be the woman promising to spend the rest of her life under his thumb. "I'm getting ready for a bridesmaids' luncheon. Is there a problem you wanted to talk over?" Her voice was polite, but any warmth was intentionally absent. She continued the task he'd interrupted, slicing vegetables for a molded salad, not daring to let down her guard for even a second.

"Why are you being so suspicious?" He nabbed a celery stalk, all the while smiling knowingly as though he saw through her indifferent act. "I promised I'd check with you when I got back in town and that's what I'm doing. Are there any decisions still hanging?" He leaned against the cabinet, ankles crossed, tasseled loafers anchoring him at a comfortable angle.

"I should hope every decision has been made," she answered peevishly. "The wedding's only five days away." She moved in front of him to take a carton of sour cream from the refrigerator.

Suddenly he said, "Would you like to grab a late breakfast?"

Amy had expected anything but this invitation. Startled, she stared up at him. "I don't think that would be a good idea, do you? Besides, I have that luncheon in a few hours." *Can't you just leave me alone?*

Max had shocked himself as much as Amy by asking her to breakfast. The only excuse he could make was that exhaustion had affected his judgment. He'd detoured by her place on his way home from the airport for a quick update, nothing more. The business trip had been successful, but he was tired to the bone after a series of sixteen- to eighteen-hour workdays. He'd merely dropped by to make sure there were no glitches to handle. He certainly hadn't meant to give the impression he was coming on to her.

He remembered her earlier comment about "toying with the hired help." Now she'd be convinced he'd done precisely that. Maybe he had acted chummier than he should have. Why, he didn't know. It just seemed to happen. And it was up to him to see that it—whatever "it" was—didn't happen again. Max resolved on the spot that his involvement with Amy Holt would be kept to a minimum from here on out.

There would be no more phone calls monitoring her progress ... Max knew Robin could rightly claim those calls weren't all business. He'd used them as a respite from work and had found in Amy a person who shared an interest in an amazing number of topics. But end of sharing. If he needed a respite, he'd talk with his future wife. And if their wedding needed discussing with Amy, he'd leave those details to Robin and live with the results, no matter what.

Days went by without Max contacting Amy again. Considering the awkwardness of their last encounter, she was glad he hadn't. Now if only there were some way to purge him from her thoughts. But it wasn't going to be easy. She might be free of his physical presence and those telephone conversations, but she couldn't escape entirely.

"Robin called while you were out," Stephanie said, handing Amy a pink message slip.

"What did she want this time?" Amy sighed.

"She didn't say. Probably wants to change the color scheme from lime green to mint green," Stephanie guessed.

Robin had phoned several times, that too frequent whine of hers setting Amy's teeth on edge like fingernails scraping a chalkboard. Robin kept fine-tuning the wedding arrangements with a series of superficial changes that accomplished little, other than adding work for Amy.

The more she was exposed to the young woman, the more persuaded Amy became that Robin Porter wouldn't hold the interest of someone like Max for long. There were no displays of wit or intellect or creative thought. Of course, it could be that none of those omissions mattered to Max. Robin was a gorgeous woman. Perhaps all he sought was a decorative ornament on his arm or a mate willing and able to produce attractive children.

Handing Amy the morning paper, Stephanie pointed to a three-inch column. "Guess who?"

Amy knew the answer without looking. Max and Robin were constantly in the society pages being feted at party upon party, celebrations hosted by friends and associates.

"Obviously Mr. Evans has given up the battle for low-profile nuptials," Steph said.

"Yes," Amy answered. "He might be able to restrain Robin, but he can't conquer all of Houston. The marriage is receiving the full measure of hoopla, regardless of Max's wishes."

Robin was probably enjoying a touch of retribution right now. On the plus side for Amy, Torrence Place had been mentioned several times and as a result, a number of inquiries had come in relative to future bookings.

Amy hadn't become involved with clients to this extent before and she emitted a silent thank-you when her appointment book showed that soon the painful association would end. Hopefully, her schoolgirl crush on Max would disappear at the same time. Today was Wednesday; she had only to get through tonight's rehearsal, then the ceremony and reception tomorrow. By the weekend she'd relegate Max Evans and his bride to the past and return to business as usual.

The rehearsal went off without a hitch. No complaints, no changes, and—surprise, surprise—Robin had even managed to cork that whine of hers. Now there was only one more day.

The sky was still dark with a luminous ivory moon visible from her window when Amy awoke to the sounds of an insistent alarm the next morning. *Oh, no, not time to get up already*! She slapped at the snooze button, then lay there, her mind starting to function, but her body rebelling. The alarm sounded again and Amy dragged herself off to the shower.

An hour later, she sat in the kitchen, slowly sipping coffee, trying to fully wake up. Amy was not a morning person and the idea of crawling out of the covers before six a.m. was sheer torture. It was one of the reasons she'd left her public relations job and gambled on being her own boss and setting her own hours. As breathtaking as sunrises might be to the eye, few people actually wanted to get married then. So it was only on rare occasions like this, when the preparations were more complicated than usual, that she had to rise before dawn.

Another hour and three cups of coffee later, Amy was hard at work dressed in tailored brown slacks, a crisp white cotton shirt, and a cooking apron. Her hair was held back with an enameled barrette, her only jewelry plain gold hoops.

Despite Robin's inclination toward overblown opulence, the wedding promised to be a lovely affair. Robin and Max would stay the night and tomorrow Amy would be rid of them forever. *Hallelujah*! Maybe then she'd regain her sanity. But first things first.

The morning passed smoothly. Amy managed to keep her thoughts about Max under control and treat the wedding as she would any other. Torrence Place had never looked so good, the dark woods rubbed to a fine luster, the crystal chandeliers sparkling.

Max arrived midafternoon, nodded a curt hello and disappeared upstairs. *Ingrate*. After all she'd done to get this wedding together, he could at least have shown some appreciation.

On second thought, I should be the grateful one. This was just the ticket for reinforcing her resolve. Another of those reality checks she'd been dependent upon lately to keep her head clear about Max Evans.

Amy heard the clock chime the half hour. It was three-thirty and in thirty minutes the wedding was to begin. Everyone had arrived—the groom, the best man, the maid of honor, ushers, friends, and members of both families. Everyone but the bride.

"You mean, she's still not here?" Max barked at Amy from the door of the Hearts and Flowers Suite. It was ten past four and she'd come to inquire whether to start the music.

"Do you think something is wrong?"

Max stroked his chin. "Shouldn't be." He picked up the telephone and dialed one number, then another. "No answer at her apartment and her cellular phone is apparently turned off. She must be on the way. Otherwise, someone would have let us know." He shook his head. "I knew Robin had developed tardiness into a fine art, but I hardly expected her to be late for her own wedding." The look he gave Amy was one of pure exasperation.

"I'm positive she'll be here any second," Amy said in a tone she employed to pacify her clients in their anxious moments. She hoped it wouldn't fail her now and that it would serve to relax the bridegroom until his fiancée showed up. "In the meantime, shall I have the violinists play?"

"At the moment, the violinists are the least of my concerns, Ms. Holt. That's your decision, so handle it."

Don't take your hostility out on me, Amy wanted to scream. She choked back the impulse. "I'll stall the musicians for a while," she replied coolly.

As Amy descended the stairs into the parlor, Stephanie rushed over to her. "What's going on?"

Amy sighed loudly. "I haven't a clue. I tried to get some guidance from Max on what to do, and instead had my head bitten off. What's the scene outside?"

"The natives are getting restless. Reverend Hulse alternates between meditating in the gazebo and soothing two sets of skittish parents. Everyone else is having a field day speculating about the delay."

"Do they all know what the problem is? That Robin's not here?"

"Yup. I even heard one of the ushers taking bets on her estimated time of arrival."

Amy glanced nervously toward the front door. "Could there have been an accident?"

"We'd have gotten word of an accident," Stephanie said in the same soft voice Amy had used with Max.

"I hope you're right. She *is* going to arrive, isn't she?"

"Of course she is. No woman would leave Max Evans in the lurch. And no sane woman would keep him waiting without a very good reason. Robin should have donned her wedding gown and been walking down the aisle by now."

"We're past aisle walking," Amy said. "The happy bride and groom should already be cutting the cake and toasting the future. The ceremony was to begin a half hour ago."

"So what do we do?"

"Perhaps we—" Amy paused at the sound of a car door slamming. She rushed to the window and pulled back the lace curtains. "It's the limo. Stephanie," she said, "go tell the musicians to start playing. I'll hurry

Robin into the Bride's Room and let the groom know she's here. With luck, this wedding will be under way in the next ten minutes.''

Max, too, heard the car door slam and glanced out the window to see Robin step casually from the car. She was dressed in an oversize shirt and leggings, her wedding dress draped over her arm. The chauffeur lifted an overnight bag from the car's trunk and followed Robin up the walk, Robin's relaxed stroll indicating she hadn't a care in the world.

Max felt like dashing outside and throttling the woman. Didn't Robin comprehend that today was special and certainly not the occasion to manufacture an attention-getting "entrance"? She was the bride, for Pete's sake, destined to be the center of attention anyway.

Almost from the moment of his proposal, Max had asked himself whether he'd done the right thing. He'd dismissed those doubts as the "cold feet" of a long-term bachelor. He honestly wanted to settle down, to have a wife and family. Now he wondered if that desire had destroyed his common sense. Was he about to make the biggest mistake of his life? Max didn't want a sham of a marriage. He wanted the "till death do us part" kind of union.

Robin had barely reached the front porch when he bounded down to meet her. "Are you all right?"

"Of course," she answered, acting nonplussed at his question. "I'm just running a little behind, that's all— what with the hairdresser and makeup artist and manicurist." She waved perfect pink nails in his direction.

"Well, at least you're okay." The muscles in Max's jaw clenched and unclenched. "Now we need to talk. Upstairs!" He grabbed Robin's arm and hustled her inside.

Amy stared uncomprehendingly, then regained her composure. She raced after them, only to be stopped in her tracks by the slamming of the door to the suite. *Darn!* Nothing had gone smoothly since the first second she'd set eyes on these two. And now this—all those guests cooling their heels outside and the principal players in conference. What was happening in there anyway? She stood in the hall frantically tapping her foot and quelling the urge to put an eye to the old-fashioned keyhole.

Interminable minutes passed, then the door opened. Robin came out, stopping in front of Amy. "I never did want to get married here anyway," she huffed. "I told Max this house had bad vibes, but he wouldn't listen. Well, other people will soon see that I knew what I was talking about. Here," she said, shoving the plastic-encased wedding gown into Amy's arms. "Put this in your next garage sale." Without another word, Robin sailed down the stairs and out the front door.

Amy didn't know whether to pursue her or to go to Max. She was seized by the dreaded realization that Robin had made good on her threat and pulled the plug on the wedding. Or had Max? That seemed more likely at the moment. He'd been mad enough to chew nails. But surely Robin would have reacted differently if Max had been the one responsible. In the brief glimpse she'd gotten, Amy'd detected no tears, more a haughty contempt.

Whatever had occurred between them, she needed to know. A garden full of people waited expectantly for a wedding to take place. With tentative steps, Amy entered Max's suite.

"Ah, Ms. Holt, come in." Max's mussed hair showed the effects of repeated finger rakings and his tux tie was undone. "My...fiancée...and I have had a change of heart." He opened his palm to display the gaudy engagement ring, then gave her a strained smile. "Unless you've got a substitute bride handy, I suppose this means the wedding's off."

CHAPTER THREE

AMY stared at him in astonishment. Sure Max and Robin were an impossible couple, but even yesterday they had appeared committed—or resigned at least—to getting married. So who or what was to blame for this startling about-face?

"Ms. Holt, are you listening? I just said the wedding's off. I'll need your support to contend with the mob out there, a mob which will be demanding explanations. As far as everyone's concerned, I'm incommunicado. Bring Aaron up here so I can ask him to make my excuses."

She nodded and ran to locate Aaron West, Max's best man. Now wasn't the time for an in-depth analysis. Action was required. Emergency action.

As soon as she'd dispatched Aaron to Max, Amy hurried to the kitchen and called to Stephanie. Quickly summarizing matters, she sent Stephanie to summon the rest of the staff. Aaron had already enlisted aid from the minister and ushers, before parking himself at the foot of the stairs to prevent anyone's attempting to see Max.

A short while later most of the gathering had dispersed. Reverend Hulse had assisted by comforting the families and diplomatically answering questions from the curious. But now even the good reverend's patience was being tested.

Stewart and Bitsy Porter, Robin's parents, were in the dining room, Stewart glowering menacingly in the direction of the Evanses and shaking a fist at Max's father.

"What's your boy gone and done to my baby? I tell you I won't let him get away with treating her the way he did Lucy Walsh. Do you hear me, Evans? I won't stand for my girl being left at the altar." Stewart Porter slammed a fist against the dining table, accidentally connecting with a layer of the flower-bedecked wedding cake. Gooey icing covered his hand and a white sugar rose stuck precariously to a finger, but he seemed oblivious to it as he continued his ranting.

"Need I remind you who held this shindig up?" Ed Evans roared back. "If anyone was left at the altar, it sure as heck wasn't Robin. My son was here as promised, ready and waiting for the 'I do's.'" As the two men belligerently stepped closer to one another, Reverend Hulse inserted himself between them, talking conciliation and calling for cooler heads. Within moments he was successfully escorting the Porters to their car.

Aaron had managed to keep visitors away from Max, including a relentless society reporter who'd conceded to interviews out on the front lawn. But Aaron gave up his barrier when Max's mother started upstairs. Margaret Evans wasn't about to be deterred from talking to her son. She didn't stay long before reappearing to confer with her husband on the landing. Both parents emerged from their huddle somber-faced, coming downstairs rather than seeking any more conversation with their son.

After the Evans family left, Reverend Hulse and Aaron soon followed, only the staff remaining to attend to the dismantling of the decorations and removal of the chairs and accessories from the garden.

Amy was in the dining room, shaking her head and wondering where to stash the wrecked wedding cake when Stephanie joined her.

"I just looked out front. That reporter's got a photographer with her."

"She sure didn't waste any time." Amy grimaced. "Negative publicity's all we need right now. The groom is upstairs in who-knows-what kind of mood. If he comes down and spots that camera, he'll probably kick both of them off the premises.

"Not that he can make the situation much worse for us. Imagine what kind of coverage this fiasco's going to receive. I can see the headlines already. 'Evans Wedding Fizzles At Eleventh Hour.' And to think I believed a high-profile ceremony was just what my business needed. What a laugh! By the time the newspapers and television stations finish with us, no one will want to have anything to do with Torrence Place or 'Arrangements by Amy.'" Amy's face fell as the realization took hold. "Go ahead and hang a shroud over the front. We're dead. We'll be labeled a jinx. I'll end up filing bankruptcy—"

Stephanie gave her a sympathetic pat on the shoulder. "Settle down. No one's going to fault you for this. Anyway, even if we do have to weather an occasional joke and a couple of cancellations, there are enough weddings already lined up to compensate."

"If they don't *all* cancel."

Amy's comment was dismissed with a wave of Stephanie's hand. "They won't—it's too time-consuming for them to start all over. Now stop worrying and tell me what to do about that reporter. Do we make a statement?"

Amy shook her head. "That's really not our job. We should probably refer her to the Porters or Max's parents."

"Do *they* know what went wrong?"

"You'll have to ask someone else that question. I'm not sure who knows what."

"Was it because Robin was late? Or because of this Lucy Walsh, whoever she is?"

"I haven't the foggiest idea. Maybe Max and Robin simply got a case of stage fright. They might change their minds back tomorrow." Why, Amy wondered, did that idea repel her so, when it should have had the opposite effect? A resurrected Porter-Evans marriage would be aggravation galore, but much better for the image of "Arrangements by Amy."

"What else do I need to do?" Stephanie asked.

"Help me put this cake away and that's it."

The two of them carried the cake into the pantry then Stephanie untied her apron and hung it on a peg. "Jay's off until Sunday and we're going to run down to Galveston. Maybe you'd feel better to get away. Want to come along?"

"You *are* a dear, Steph, but I have no interest in being a third wheel." The heavy demands of Jay Anders's medical residency and Stephanie's two jobs often had them bemoaning their limited hours together. "You've done enough." Amy gave her a hug. "Thanks for everything. Now go off to frolic with Jay while I figure out some way to deal with the reporter."

Amy breathed easier as the reporter and cameraman drove away. She glanced at the grandfather clock in the foyer. In less than an hour she'd managed to remove all traces of the event—the people departed, the kitchen cleaned, the decorations removed, the gourmet buffet and wedding cake out of sight, and the dining room vacuumed. Amy knew Max didn't need any mementos of the wedding that almost was.

She had just turned to go and tell him that the coast was clear when he appeared at the top of the stairs and started down. He looked around. "Very efficient, Ms.

Holt. I even spotted you getting rid of the news hound. You're a resourceful woman."

All well and good, but all Amy wanted was to be resourceful enough to get him out of her hair, then treat herself to a hot bath and a couple of aspirin and try to recover from this ill-fated afternoon.

She wished she could tell from his expression exactly how Max was reacting. Surely he was unhappy. How could he not be? Yet from all outward appearances, calling off his wedding seemed no more than a minor inconvenience. In fact, Max almost looked as though he couldn't care less.

This made no sense to Amy. No one would go to so much time and effort—to say nothing of the expense— if he didn't want to get married. And, even if Max wasn't all that much in love, it had to be a personal embarrassment to back down at the crucial moment. Obviously he was putting on a show of male bravado.

Fine with her, Amy decided. If that was his way of handling the problem, his way of preserving his dignity, she wouldn't undermine the endeavor. She'd just negotiate the few remaining details and he could be on his way. As Max came closer, she said to him, "The food, Mr. Evans. If you've no objection, we could—"

"Dump it."

"I had a homeless shelter in mind—"

"Okay, if you think they'll want it, but I suspect they'd prefer something more substantial like meat and potatoes. Speaking of meat and potatoes, I'm starved. How about rustling up a meal?"

"Here?"

"Is that so strange? You were prepared to serve a hundred people an hour ago. Call whomever you please about the party food, but in the meantime, let's raid the refrigerator." He clasped her shoulders and turned her toward the kitchen.

Amy opened the refrigerator door and stared at the containers inside. "Would you rather have Swedish meatballs or some of the crab canapés?"

"I was hoping for real food. A sandwich, for instance." He gripped the top of the refrigerator door with one hand and leaned over Amy to peer at the array of jars and boxes.

"Roast beef okay?" she asked, wishing he would give her breathing room.

"Fine." Max dropped his hand, but didn't back away. "How about a real drink, too? Didn't I order an open bar? I'd prefer something stronger than that champagne over in the corner." He motioned to the plastic coolers filled with ice and bottles of Dom Pérignon, the only thing she'd neglected to put away.

"Your erstwhile bride-to-be did a thumbs-down on the bar. Don't you remember?" Amy pulled out sandwich fixings and a delicatessen package of beef, then moved around Max to the butcher-block countertop. "She wanted something more elegant than 'whisky and beer.'" Inadvertently, Amy's voice slipped into an imitation of Robin's high-pitched tone.

He closed the refrigerator door and turned to face her. "Do I detect disapproval of my almost-bride?"

"I—" Amy paused. *What could she say?* Whatever her opinion of Robin and no matter what had caused this breakup, she had no right to mock Max's fiancée. "I didn't mean to be judgmental. Champagne *is* more elegant for a wedding reception." She opened a cabinet door to reveal a selection of liquor. After what had transpired this afternoon, she understood Max needing a drink—she wouldn't mind one herself. "It's just that I can't help feeling bad," she continued. "All that work, all that trouble. For nothing."

"You got paid," he said, reaching for a bottle of Scotch. "Rather well as I recall."

"Is money all you ever think about?" She should have known better than to offer words of sympathy to Max. He seemed to have dollar signs for brain cells, managing to interpret every word from her as financially motivated. Then she remembered his state of mind and decided to make allowances. "Mix yourself a cocktail while I get a napkin and place mat for the dining table."

"Only one?" Max asked. "Don't tell me you're going to make me eat alone? And on that big formal dining table? The one Stew Porter pounded, probably wishing it were my jaw."

"So you heard about that?"

"My mother told me." He took a glass from the cabinet and filled it with ice. "Would you like a drink?"

"White wine." Amy couldn't help wondering what *else* his mother had told him about the altercation with Robin's parents and decided she had nothing to lose by asking. "Who's Lucy Walsh?"

Max sighed.

"Please don't tell me it's none of my business. In view of the fact there was almost a fistfight in my dining room, I think I have a right to know."

He sighed again. "All right," he said resignedly. "I guess it's no big secret. Lucy's probably one of the reasons I didn't call off this farce weeks ago."

Farce. Interesting comment, Amy thought and wondered if his cynical description was hurt feelings in disguise. She took down a second place mat and completed setting the table, in the kitchen where it'd be more conducive to conversation. "So?" she prodded, when Max didn't offer more information.

"When I was in college I dated Lucy for a semester. Then without warning, she announced to the world we were engaged. It wasn't true. I'd never mentioned marriage, much less proposed. But she'd concluded that our dating exclusively meant a commitment. Maybe it did, but not the kind she was thinking about. Things got pretty sticky and there was no gracious way out. She accused me of making a laughingstock of her, dropped out of school and bummed around Europe for a year. Most people believed I'd broken a pledge and also poor Lucy's heart." Max's mouth curved downward in a troubled grimace.

"So what does that have to do with Robin?" Amy finished making their sandwiches, then carried the plates to the table.

Politely Max seated her and took his own place, unfolding a linen napkin and spreading it across his lap. "Perhaps this was an instance where I was too concerned about appearances and not concerned enough about reality. I had already been painted as the bad guy once. What would I have been labeled if I'd seemingly ducked out for a second time?"

"You may find out the answer to that question."

The frown intensified. "So be it. I'm tired of dwelling on it." He took a bite of sandwich. "This is great. I'm even hungrier than I realized. Amazing what not getting married can do for the appetite," he said, speaking like a man reprieved rather than a disappointed one.

For a while they ate in silence, then Max glanced over her way. "Considering this is a workroom, your kitchen is very cozy. As a matter of fact, I like the whole house."

"Thanks," Amy said with a flash of pride, pleased by the compliment and amazed at the facility with which Max could put his unhappiness aside and exchange pleasantries over a meal.

He dabbed his mouth with his napkin. "How did you come to own Torrence Place?"

"In a way it fell into my lap. This was my grand-parents' home, part of the estate inherited by my mother. My parents maintained ownership for a while and rented it out. But after moving to Dallas, they found being absentee landlords a headache. When they decided to put the property on the market, I got this brainstorm to buy it. Typical parents, they refused to sell . . . insisted on giving the house to me. The only stipulation was that I use my purchase money to restore Torrence Place to its old glory."

"Sounds like a good deal. Heights properties are in demand—it's not often anything along the boulevard is available. You got quite a bargain."

"Originally, I thought so too. But the project was more extensive than they or I ever dreamed—replacing the roof, the plumbing, the wiring . . . and that was only the beginning."

He nodded knowingly. "You're saying you got in over your head."

"Well at least up to my eyeballs." She almost said more, but stopped herself. So it had taken all her savings plus some hefty loans to make Torrence Place the show-piece it was becoming? So she agonized about finances on a daily basis? That was her problem. She didn't intend to share the particulars of her dismal financial condition with Max Evans, especially when taking into account his profession. Max bought and sold real estate, and Torrence Place was a valuable property.

Numerous companies had sought her out about listing it. Despite the fact he specialized in large commercial ventures, Max himself might be motivated to latch on to a plum such as Torrence Place. After all, this area was practically in the shadows of the downtown skyscrapers with every square inch coveted by developers. If Max realized the extent of her money woes, he might start pressuring her to sell her home—and at outlet mall prices. Amy didn't want the hassle.

"Another sandwich?" she asked, changing the subject. When he declined, she picked up her plate and moved toward the sink.

Max gave her what appeared to be a supportive smile as she came back for his plate. "Getting started in anything is expensive, especially with the kind of quality workmanship you put into the house. You must have had to borrow heavily."

The man refuses to be deterred, Amy thought, irritated now at his nosy insightfulness, as well as for overstaying his welcome. She was more than ready for him to leave. Maybe if she gave him a taste of his own medicine, probed into his own sensitive matters, Max would become uncomfortable and decide to go. Since the first day he had walked into Torrence Place with Robin, Amy'd been curious about him. Now she had a rationalization for meddling. "Why were you marrying Robin?"

Only a blink of his blue eyes gave any indication she'd disconcerted him. His voice was steady when he answered, "I'm not sure that's any of your concern."

"Indulge me, then. After all, I have been caught up in this... I believe you used the word *farce*." *It was past the point for diplomacy.* "So why?"

"It's rather complicated."

"Your biological clock was ticking down?" Amy asked sarcastically.

"Oh, I think biology's allotted me several more years. Could be I was tired of the constant badgering, friends and family vigorously hinting it was getting kind of late. Everyone I know subscribes to Jane Austen's premise that 'a single man in possession of a good fortune must be in want of a wife.' They were driving me crazy trying to fix me up."

"So you thought it easier to get married than endure the pressure?" Amy refreshed Max's drink, then rejoined him at the table. "Surely you were capable of handling a bunch of frustrated Cupids," she said. "There's got to be more to it than that."

"A lot of reasons contributed to my decision. True, there *was* the pressure. And the age thing, too. I decided the time had come to make a commitment. As you've implied, I'm now closer to forty than thirty. My parents and two sisters all have a happy family life and they'd like to see me settled down. I'd like that, too. As much as I adore my nieces and nephews, I want children of my own."

"So you picked Robin." *Even though none of your reasons had anything to do with falling in love.*

"It seemed a good choice at the time." *It had,* Max reminded himself silently, tired of trying to explain—to justify—his actions to this snip of a female. He and Robin ran in the same social whirl, had mutual friends, liked sports and the arts. Too, he didn't have to question whether she was marrying him for himself or his money since she had plenty of her own.

Importantly he'd been attracted to her—for a while. But when or how the relationship started unraveling, he wasn't certain. *Where did I go wrong?* "I was convinced I'd weighed every angle." His thoughts slipped out.

"Did it ever occur to you that you might have approached marriage in a convoluted way?" Amy took advantage of the opening to continue cross-examining Max. "Weighing 'angles' instead of emotions?"

"It does now," he said. "Is that what you want to hear?"

"All I care about is hearing the truth—the whole truth."

Suddenly Max raised his eyebrows up and down. "Even if the *whole* truth might be that I fell for someone else. You, for instance."

Amy self-consciously gulped the remainder of her wine. "Spare me," she said.

"You mean you're dismissing out of hand that I've come to care for you. Rather heartless I should say."

"Enough of this silliness." Amy should have known he'd seize the conversation and turn it disconcertingly his way. "Let's talk about something else."

"Sure," he said, unperturbed. Resting his elbows on the table, he studied her. "Let's see...as I remember, we were discussing Torrence Place. A lot of talent went into restoring those old oak moldings. You've done a heads-up job with the furnishings, too. The house is really lovely."

"Thank you," Amy said warily. Not once in his previous visits had Max mentioned the surroundings, yet tonight he'd practically turned into an interior designer. She didn't know what to make of this conversational gambit.

"I must admit I'm happy with the way it's turning out," she volunteered cautiously. "Still, the upstairs is not nearly finished—only the two suites. I've closed off the rest for now."

"Well, what you have completed is perfect. I normally prefer more contemporary furniture, but the antiques you've acquired are just right." He leaned back and clasped his hands behind his head. "Yes, as long as I have to hole up somewhere for a week or so, this is as good a place as I could hope to find."

"What?" Amy gasped, rising to her feet. Surely she hadn't heard correctly. "What do you mean?" she managed somewhat more calmly, even though her voice squeaked tellingly.

"Exactly what I said. The smartest thing is for me to hide out here. One reporter's already got the story on today's debacle. A dozen'll soon follow. I'm not inclined to talk to any news types just yet and this is probably the last place they'd look."

"Well, I'm sorry," she said, propping her hands on the table and leaning toward him, "you'll have to find somewhere else to 'hide out.' Torrence Place isn't a sanctuary. Or a hotel."

"Really?" He tilted farther back in his chair, stretching out his legs, his relaxed posture a contrast to the obstinacy in his eyes. "The package does include a honeymoon stay."

"Sure." Amy's spine became ruler straight. "One night for the bride and groom in the Hearts and Flowers Suite. That doesn't mean we accommodate overnight guests on a regular basis."

"I'm not talking about a year's lease—just a few days, and the 'Hearts and Flowers' is fine. My luggage is still up there so I'm all set."

"I told you..." Amy paused and counted to ten. "We don't cater to sleeping guests."

"Oh, I doubt I'll be doing a lot of sleeping. Actually..." His eyes met hers in challenge. "My earlier plans didn't include sleeping at all."

"You should have kept that in mind before you sent the bride away."

"What makes you think I sent her away? Maybe she was the one who did a turnabout. Surely you can muster a bit of compassion for a jilted bridegroom."

"Are you sure you're the injured party?" Amy's attitude conveyed skepticism. All threats to the contrary, she simply couldn't believe that Robin was the one who'd terminated the proceedings.

"For the sake of argument, let's just say it was a joint decision. And stop trying to cast me as the villain. Did Robin seem brokenhearted when she left?"

"No," Amy admitted. "But she was here...ready to—"

"She was ridiculously late. Not particularly anxious to plight her troth." Max massaged the back of his neck. "Look...I'm too weary to spar with you anymore. Can't we save the rest of this conversation for tomorrow?"

"You won't be here tomorrow. I'll be glad to refund your lodging costs."

"A refund on my honeymoon? No way. I paid for a wedding night and that's what I intend to have." His expression was stubborn and it also held something else, something Amy couldn't define. The way he was staring at her right now, she was positive he wasn't thinking of Robin. Suddenly Torrence Place seemed terribly confining.

Laughing, he stood up and moved closer.

"What's so amusing?" Amy asked, gritting her teeth, self-conscious and aggravated that she'd given her emotions away. She could feel the betraying heat of that blush on her cheeks again.

"Were you afraid I'd suggest that you join me upstairs?" He gently stroked his knuckles across her chin. "Never fear. I plan to spend the night alone. Although it is an awfully big bed for one person."

She could tell he was teasing; nevertheless, Amy's discomfort worsened.

He put his hand on her shoulder. "Listen, all I want is refuge from the media. To remain here until the coast is clear."

She tried to instill some authority in her voice. "The press is persistent. They'll keep hunting for you. You should talk to them . . . issue a statement or something and get it over with."

"I'm not up to statements. Later perhaps, but not now. In the meantime, I won't be booted out."

What's the use, she thought. He'd made it clear he wasn't budging, so she might as well go easy on herself and concede the skirmish—but not the war. Max was going, whether he liked it or not. She went to the cabinet and pulled out a bottle of cognac. "Care for an after-dinner drink?" With luck, the alcohol would mellow him enough that she could persuade him to leave.

Max accepted the glass of brandy and took an evaluative swallow.

"Wouldn't you be more comfortable at home?" Amy asked, making one last-ditch try.

"Are you on that again? Haven't I made it crystal clear I'm settling in?" He spoke slowly and precisely as if correcting a willful child.

Their eyes locked for several moments before Amy gave up. "Okay," she said with resignation, "you're welcome to stay for tonight. But beyond then is out of the question."

Max turned, glass in hand, and started for the stairs. "We'll see."

CHAPTER FOUR

AMY trailed after him. "I'm afraid I must put my foot down," she called to his back. "I have another wedding on Sunday and I need the weekend to prepare." She hoped he recognized the determination in her tone. "Besides, I distinctly recollect that you were to depart before noon tomorrow on your honeymoon trip. Where was it you were going?"

Max leaned over the banister, his brandy snifter in his hands, his eyes twinkling in contentious amusement. "To Maui. Why do you ask?"

At that moment, gazing up into those dancing, now-lavender eyes, Amy wondered what could have possessed Robin Porter to let this man get away. He was more than handsome, there was an aura about him that couldn't be ignored. Magnetic was the most apt description, clichéd though it was. *What's wrong with me,* she asked herself, *getting mush-brained over some guy who happens to come wrapped in a pretty package?* Her objective at the moment was to be rid of Max Evans, not tumble for him.

"Maui," she repeated placatingly. "A great spot to hide out. Much better than Torrence Place. Surely no reporters would look for you there." Max Evans might be hot stuff in Texas, but in Hawaii, he'd simply be another tourist.

Max's eyebrows moved together in a quizzical frown. "What in heaven's name would I do in Maui now? A honeymoon trip by myself? I don't think so." He straightened and took a sip of his brandy. "Why don't you come with me?" he challenged.

"Gee, I'm sorry," she said insincerely, "but I've already made plans. Remember, I've got a wedding to tend to."

"So instead I'll hang around and help you. Then we'll head to Maui. I'll just book a later flight."

"Hold it. I'm not going to Maui...I'm not going anywhere with you." *Unless it's to drive you home.*

He shrugged. "No problem. We just revert to Plan A. I stay here."

Darn. She should have let him retire to bed and continued this discussion in the morning when, if the Fates were kinder, both of them would be in a better frame of mind. She'd hoped for a little relaxation during the next day or so. Until she got Max out of her way, relaxing would be impossible.

Amy scowled, a wasted effort she knew, but the only action she could come up with other than calling the police to haul him out. Now that would be a pretty picture for sensation-seeking paparazzi. *Admit it*, she told herself. *You're completely boxed in.* "Then stay!" she shrieked. "But tonight's it. I want you packed and gone tomorrow." She didn't wait for his response.

After tidying the kitchen, Amy headed gratefully for the part of Torrence Place she considered hers and hers alone—a suite at the rear of the house consisting of bedroom, sitting room and a large, luxurious bath. Finally she was going to get that soak—a long one in her grandmother's old claw-footed bathtub. Lots of hot water and bubbles. It had been a taxing day. Thank heaven the next wedding would be a small one.

Momentarily, all thoughts of the Porter-Evans disaster and of Max Evans himself waned and she reflected on the people getting married at noon on Sunday—Eva

Brown and Ralph Jennings, both nearing eighty. Amy occasionally volunteered at a local retirement center and it was there she'd met the two. It pleased her to see how they'd giggled like teenagers when they told her about their romance. Later when they asked to be married at Torrence Place, she was thrilled.

Whenever she visualized their wedding, Amy felt a spurt of happiness. This union proved to her that love had no barriers of time. It could happen at any age.

The gathering would include a short service, then lunch for approximately twenty guests. Eva and Ralph lived on Social Security and had asked only for a bare-bones ceremony, to be followed by a cake and punch reception. Amy had insisted on adding lunch, as her gift to them. Ironically, Sunday's festivities would have the simplicity Max himself had sought.

All through her bath and the nightly ritual of preparing for bed, Amy's mind kept reverting to Max's wedding. *Why had it self-destructed like that*? She lay curled on her side, head resting on her folded hands, still fixated on the topic. If everything had proceeded on course, right now Robin would be upstairs with Max, her new husband. He would be kissing her and holding her and... The room was suddenly too warm. Amy kicked the sheet aside.

For moments she continued lying there, longing for slumber, yet knowing it wouldn't come. Then she remembered her novel. No wonder she was having trouble falling asleep. Her insomnia had nothing to do with Max. She was accustomed to dozing off with a book and the one she'd started was on the desk in her office.

Amy padded down the hall to retrieve the novel and was about to turn off the office lamp when Max sauntered in. He'd undressed and now wore a burgundy silk robe with matching pajama bottoms. The sash of the robe hung loose, and unwillingly Amy found herself staring at a strong, broad chest, at muscles that rippled down his torso. *Personal trainer, no doubt. One who definitely earns his wages.*

It took a moment for her to realize she was gawking and raise her eyes, only to discover that Max was also staring—and seeing a great deal more than she. Used to being alone, Amy hadn't grabbed a robe—all she wore was a flimsy pair of shortie pajamas.

She stood rigid as though welded to the floor. Max broke the spell. "I decided I needed another drink," he explained as he secured the sash of his robe, all the while his eyes focused on her. Eventually he looked away. "It may take a lot of brandy to get me through the night. Especially now," he added softly as he turned and exited from the room.

It's every bit as bad as I feared. Amy sat at the kitchen table engrossed in the morning newspaper. She'd expected coverage in the social columns, possibly even a small news item, but definitely not anything like this piece at the bottom of the front page. Not only did the reporter give chapter and verse of yesterday's doings, but also went into elaborate detail about an earlier mishap at Torrence Place when the sprinkler system came on during a ceremony and doused participants and guests alike. The implication was that offbeat occurrences were a regular feature.

Then, to add insult to injury, the paper included a companion photo, a dreary old pre-renovation picture of Torrence Place, resembling something only the Addams Family would want to call home.

Amy retrieved her appointment calendar from the office and reviewed the scheduled weddings. She was booked as far ahead as Valentine's Day of next year, deposits already in hand. But deposits didn't guarantee a wedding would take place. There could be some backing out. A premonition told her there would be, especially if Robin spread her "bad vibes" opinion too widely. Amy went over to the cabinet and pulled out a bottle of aspirin. Aspirin was becoming her new best friend since Max Evans entered her life.

"May I have a couple of those?"

Amy turned around and experienced a twinge of guilt at her self-absorption. The consequences of Thursday might be traumatic for her, but obviously they were much worse for Max, whose appearance suggested someone who'd been on a three-day bender.

His hair was uncombed, his unshaven face had a bilious cast to it and there were dark circles under his rather glassy eyes. Only his pressed jeans and neat navy T-shirt indicated any semblance of order, and bilious or not, he was still extraordinarily handsome.

She filled a tumbler with ice cubes and water, handed the glass to Max and spilled two of the tablets into his palm.

"Thanks. And don't say it . . . I know I look like hell."

Under less difficult circumstances Amy might have commented "Rough night?" Now such an utterance would come off as mean-spirited. Besides, she remembered all too vividly Max's suggestive innuendos from the previous evening and refused to risk sending the conversation in that direction again.

Amy didn't feel like wisecracks this morning anyway, not having slept well, either, and was thankful Max hadn't noticed that she didn't look so terrific herself.

She'd spent a large part of the night thinking about being alone with Max at Torrence Place...contemplating what might have happened if they weren't in separate beds, on different floors of the house. Her book had not served its purpose and only after endless tossing and turning had she fallen into a fitful sleep, awakening more fatigued than when she'd gone to bed.

The two of them silently watched the dripping of coffee into the carafe, then Amy rose and filled china cups. "Do you care for breakfast?"

Max grimaced. "I'd better wait and see if the aspirin and coffee take hold. Of all the stupid stunts—a hangover! This hasn't happened since I was in college." He rubbed his temples. "Ouch. My head's pounding like the top'll blow off any second." He slumped over the kitchen table, pulling the morning newspaper closer.

It took only an instant for a scowl to form as he studied the picture and caption about the wedding, the frown deepening as he read the accompanying article. The article didn't say much, but the descriptions of the bewildered guests, the tardy bride, and the last-minute reversal were story enough.

Amy couldn't help but feel sorry for Max. She brought the carafe to him and freshened his coffee. "So what happens now?"

"Nothing. I sit tight and stay here . . . just like I said." He gave her a wry smile. "You didn't really think you'd get rid of me this morning, did you, Ms. Holt?" Max might have a hangover, but there was still a gleam in those bloodshot eyes.

"Oh, but I did—still do," she answered sharply, annoyed that she'd felt an ounce of concern for him. "Once those aspirin work their magic, I expect to see you packing."

"Quite the charming hostess today, aren't we? Don't overdo the welcome or it'll go to my head."

Amy thought she detected a wince at the memory of his aching head. *Serves him right*. She mixed a pitcher of orange juice and poured herself a glass, placing the crystal pitcher on the table. "You can help yourself and fix your own breakfast, too, if you decide you're hungry." She took her juice and went to her office, closing the door behind her.

With a single phone call, Amy made arrangements for disposition of the leftover wedding food. Then she jotted down a list of shopping items, grabbed her purse and left without bothering to tell Max goodbye. He was a smart man, almost as smart as he fancied himself to be. Sooner or later he'd figure out she was gone. She gave a silent prayer that by the time she returned, he'd also be gone.

The morning passed faster than Amy had anticipated as she rushed through routine errands—refueling and washing her car, a visit to the florist, stops at the dry cleaner's and grocery. Of all the people she encountered, only the florist had commented about the events of the previous day, and his words were an attempt to be encouraging. "People forget," he'd assured Amy.

I wish, Amy thought, finding no comfort in his well-meaning statement. Maybe with different players people would forget...but not with this wedding. Houston would be buzzing about the event for weeks and she feared the aftereffects.

Her fears materialized into fact when she came in the rear entry and glimpsed two telephone notes stuck to the front of her refrigerator. Max had taken the messages for her, one a cancellation and the second a request that she return the call. She stormed into the hall and ran into Max.

"Why are you still here and why were you answering *my* telephone?" she demanded, venting her frustrations.

"Just those two times," he said, ignoring the first half of her question. "I called my folks and my secretary to let them know where I was. When the telephone rang right after I'd hung up, I presumed it was one of them. I'm sorry if I caused any problems."

"No problems," she grumbled, stuffing the message slips in her pocket. "But stay off my telephone—and go home."

Suddenly his eyes strayed to a point behind her and he motioned Amy to turn around.

She did so, mortified to discover visitors in the parlor, witnesses to her explosion. *Darn his hide!* "I didn't know you had company," she said sweetly to Max.

Max smiled, clearly relishing her discomfort. "They were the ones who reminded me I'd better check in with a few people."

"Hello." Amy approached them and extended her hand. "I'm Amy Holt. Welcome to Torrence Place. May I offer you something to drink? Coffee, tea?"

"Not for me, thanks," the woman answered charmingly. "I'm Jenna Peters."

"Me, either. Roger Lipinski," the man said. "I'm chief of security at Evans Enterprises." He shook Amy's hand.

"When no one was able to tell us of Max's whereabouts," Jenna said, "we drove over to see if you could, and what do you know—here he was!" She solicitously draped an arm on Max's shoulder. "We appreciate your taking care of our boy and keeping him in line. Roger and I are both aware of what a nuisance he can be."

"Thanks for the flattering words, Jenna," Max said caustically. "But Ms. Holt doesn't need any help from you in assessing me." He shot a glance Amy's way, then turned back to Jenna. "She's quite capable of forming her own critical opinions."

So the guy is Max's security chief. But who is Jenna Peters? No one had provided a clue. Roger was fortyish and wore a wedding ring; Jenna, thirtyish, didn't, so evidently they weren't a twosome. And while Jenna had aptly expressed Amy's view about Max and although the woman seemed nothing but friendly, Amy felt strangely competitive toward her.

Amy detected in Jenna an air of protectiveness regarding Max's welfare. Or was it possessiveness in disguise? Maybe she was the first of many female predators who'd soon be stalking this fresh prey.

An awkward silence ensued with Amy deciding it best to excuse herself. "Well then, if you don't need anything, I'll just let you get on with your...with your visit."

Amy remained closeted in her office for the next hour balancing her accounts and returning the telephone call. The call wasn't a cancellation at all, merely a question about changing the ceremony from eight to seven.

Even with the office door closed, Amy could hear peals of laughter from the parlor. She was glad someone was happy. Max certainly appeared to be making a rapid recovery from any disappointment. And from all indications, Jenna wasn't terribly disappointed, either.

One would think nothing worse than a few sprinkles had fallen on yesterday's parade. There were no funereal frowns, no flowing of condolences. Was there something she didn't know about the rich and famous? Were they so different from ordinary people that a torpedoed wedding was just a minor trifle?

As Max had pointed out, Robin hadn't acted all that upset. Perhaps she was even enjoying the notoriety. The only one who seemed to care was Amy. For her, it was a terrible setback. And not just monetarily. Finances always remained secondary to what her business was really about...love. Love and romance. She took it quite seriously and was appalled to discover there were those who could view the loss of a lover so cavalierly.

She heard when Roger left and it was at least an additional thirty minutes before Jenna departed. Like Robin, this woman was beautiful. Perhaps Max had already latched on to a replacement for his fiancée. The notion made Amy even more distressed. If Max Evans had another wedding in the works when the body of the first one wasn't even cold, he could get someone else to plan it. Amy wouldn't be so masochistic as to get involved a second time.

The instant she heard the front door close, Amy was on her feet. Taking a deep breath, she cautiously eased into the hall. There were no noises. Max wasn't in the parlor. She started in the direction of the kitchen only to bump right into him.

"Oh, you're still here," she said, retreating into the dining room. "I was hoping you'd left with your lady friend." Actually she was dismayed by the idea and proud of the restraint in her voice. It had just the right tone of insouciance—almost a verbal yawn. Or so she thought. Max's response made her wonder if he was able to read her mind.

"You jealous?"

"You're mistaking aggravation for jealousy," she retorted, restraint fading fast. "I told you I don't run a hotel, but you've insisted on remaining anyway. Now you're drawing in all these people."

"Two people. Not exactly a convention." He pulled out a chair from the dining table, spun it around and straddled it, folding his arms across the top. "You're just upset because they witnessed you in the middle of a tirade." He grinned.

"It was no such thing." Yet Amy knew it was exactly that—pent-up tension spewing forth. She'd been fidgety, unsettled for longer than she cared to remember, starting about the time she first met Max Evans. And it looked as if she'd never be free of him. "But if it were a tirade," she continued, "you'd be to blame."

"Me?"

"Yes, you. If you would just go home like I asked, our lives could begin to return to normal."

"Not much chance of that happening for me," he said dryly. "Jenna and Roger were advising me not to go home. Apparently this is a slow news period and the media is using my situation as filler until something more newsworthy happens. One TV station has a truck parked in front of my parents' estate and tabloid reporters are camped in the lobby of my office building and outside the gate of my condo."

"That's too bad," Amy sympathized. "I wish I could help, but—"

"You *can* help. The question is whether you will. Look, I know I'm asking for a big favor, but I'll make it worth your while financially. What can it hurt? My hanging around for a few days or a week won't impact your business. Any damage there has already been done."

Amy knew he was right. As far as "Arrangements by Amy" was concerned, the damage *was done*. But the potential repercussions went further than her business, indeed straight to her heart. She was unwillingly attracted to Max and this close confinement could cause that attraction to intensify.

But how could she turn him out and not be guilt-ridden? What he'd asked of her wasn't so much, not from his point of view. Her only hope was that the familiarity adage might prove true and breed into a permanent Max Evans cure. And the extra money would come in handy. She propped a hand under her chin, mulling over her decision.

"So, what's your answer?" Max said, after minutes had passed.

"I guess you can," she agreed, wondering as she spoke how soon regrets would set in. "For a while."

"Well, thanks for the enthusiastic vote of confidence, Ms. Holt. I'll try to be worthy of your faith in me as a guest." He grabbed her hand for a genteel kiss.

"Okay, okay," Amy said, pulling the hand away and tucking it behind her. "Just remember that my duties don't include entertaining or consoling you."

"I suppose this is a rather new experience for you," Max said. "Consoling a groom on the loose."

"Yes, it is, and not one I'd care to repeat."

He smiled, obviously not offended by her remark. "You won't be sorry, I promise." He rose from the chair. "Now, if you'll excuse me, I think I'll try to reclaim a little of that shut-eye I lost last night."

She stifled the urge to ask him whether he was still recovering from the demon rum, then decided to leave well enough alone. "Good idea," she said, realizing she needed some time to herself to devise a strategy for ousting him. Just because she'd agreed Max could stay, didn't mean a week, as he'd asked. Two, three days maximum and he was out on his ear.

He'd said, "You won't be sorry," a pronouncement Amy met with a high degree of skepticism. She'd been sorry about every step of her association with Max and she suspected this would be no exception. As long as he was around, her whole existence would be subjected to who-knew-what kind of overwhelming influences.

Lounging in an overstuffed chair, Amy had turned on the television to watch the evening news when Max tapped on the door of her sitting room and opened it. He was freshly shaven and carried a Coca-Cola in his hand and a paperback under his arm. "So this is your inner sanctum. Mind if I join you?"

As much as Amy wanted to answer that, yes, she did mind her private space being invaded, she couldn't say so. For the time being, while he was here with her permission, she'd make an effort to be hospitable. Amy moved a pile of mail from the sofa and motioned for him to sit down, just as a shot of Torrence Place flashed on the television screen. Max grabbed the remote control from the coffee table and increased the volume.

The segment showed clips of Max and Robin at the Houston polo grounds and one of him in a hard hat at a recent ribbon cutting. "The wedding that didn't happen is shrouded in secrecy," the reporter announced. "Rumor has it that Robin Porter has fled to Mexico. But where is Max Evans?"

"Where indeed," Amy said, taking the remote from Max and switching the set off. She'd heard enough. "Shouldn't you issue a statement and curb all this speculation?"

"What could I say to end it? That we changed our minds? No one would buy such a dull explanation. People want something meatier to chew on. Besides, it hardly seems anyone's business but mine and Robin's."

Amy wondered if his last words had been another warning to her, a reminder not to pry. Well, tough. Since Max was intent on lodging here, he would have to endure her queries.

"Whether it's anyone's business is beside the point," Amy told him. "We all love to gossip. Especially about celebrities. You're a well-known man whose wedding was scrubbed in a spectacular fashion. So naturally people are talking."

"Good old human nature," he agreed cynically. "The only silver lining is that the interest will be short-lived.

Pretty soon a juicier scandal will come along to capture everyone's attention. If I'm lucky, that'll happen real fast.''

Sounded like whistling in the dark to Amy, and Max didn't act totally convinced himself. In fact, he seemed almost wistful, making her wonder what was going on in that convoluted mind of his.

"So how do you feel?" she prodded.

"Now?"

"Right now." Amy decided to cut to the chase. Maybe if persuaded to unburden himself, Max would see that his best course of action was to go home and face the press, then get on with his life. He'd have to do that sooner or later. Why not sooner?

"Hungry. That's how I feel. I haven't eaten all day. Think we could whip up another sandwich? Or order in?"

"We can arrange something," she said. "After you've answered my question."

"You'd starve a man?"

"You hardly look starved." Just the opposite, Amy mused. He looked absolutely perfect, his T-shirt framing a taut chest and stomach, his jeans hugging long muscular legs... She jerked her head, wondering how to keep those embarrassing thoughts from entering her brain. "Come on now, I want answers."

"Tenacious little thing, aren't you? Okay, what do you wish me to say? That I'm confused? That I misread Robin? That just because I was resigned to marriage didn't mean she was?"

Twenty-four hours might have passed since the canceled wedding, but Max was no more forthcoming than he'd been last night. He hadn't confessed any pangs of unrequited love or pain of disappointment. He hadn't admitted anything at all.

"Resigned to marriage—how uplifting! Just what every woman wants to hear from her beloved."

"Can we discuss supper or is this interrogation going on indefinitely?" he complained. Amy could tell her remarks had nettled him. *Good.*

"I've defrosted a quiche," she said, temporarily yielding to his wishes. "It can heat while I toss a salad."

The meal was almost over when Amy returned to "the interrogation." Max could complain all he wanted about that and about her tenacity, but Amy believed in airing out wounds rather than letting them fester. "You really didn't tell me before. Just how well are you coping?"

"Oh, we're back on that, are we? As you can see, I'm coping just fine."

"I think you're in denial. Did it occur to you that sharing your feelings might help?"

"And you're volunteering to play psychologist?" He snorted. "What are you expecting from me? To confess that I'm brokenhearted? Well, I'm not. And, as I told you before, neither is Robin."

"I'm not worried about Robin's feelings. It's—"

"*Me* you're worried about? How nice." Max's eyes were mischievous.

"I didn't say that. I'm merely trying to get you to face facts. No matter what happened in that last brief meeting between the two of you, you must be disillusioned. Angry even. I believe—"

"Tenderhearted Amy," he interrupted, dropping the pretentious Ms. Holt he'd heretofore used. "You're almost convincing me that you care."

He reached across the table and took her hand in his, altogether too familiarly for Amy. She needed to get this conversation back on an even keel. "Were you in love with Robin?" Amy purposely kept her tone modulated.

She didn't want Max to get the mistaken notion that it mattered to her whether he was or not.

He released her hand and stretched, rotating his shoulder muscles. "Ah, love. I should have known that Amy, the romantic, would get around to that sooner or later. Well, since you're obviously not going to rest until you have me baring my soul, I'll let you in on something. In all my thirty-eight years, I've never experienced that particular emotion. What's more, I'm positive I never will. Surely if there was anything to this love business, I'd have brushed against it during the past couple of decades."

Amy stood up, offended. "I find it difficult to believe that no woman has ever captured your—" She'd almost said "heart," but after his big speech, Amy doubted he had one.

"My...?" Max prompted.

She groped for the right word. "Your...your fancy." An antiquated term, nevertheless appropriate, since Max seemed to consider her beliefs outmoded, anyway.

"Oh, I've *fancied* quite a number of your fair sex. There've been chances galore for that highly revered sensation labeled love to seize me," he said with exaggerated formality. "Alas, it's never happened. Why should I expect it now at my age?"

"You talk as if you're a hundred years old." She picked up their empty plates and started toward the sink.

"Not quite, but old enough to realize that the notion of eternal love is mostly propaganda." Max got up and followed her across the kitchen, turning her to face him, cupping her elbows in his hands. He leaned close to whisper. "Did it ever occur to you that being 'in love' is like the flu? It hits you, sends you reeling, then you get over it. Fortunately, I haven't caught the bug."

Amy jerked free. "Is that why you planned your wedding like some sort of corporate merger?" She had to remember who he was—Max Evans, the consummate businessman. Just for a heartbeat, when he was touching her, she'd been tempted to forget.

"Don't shrink away," he said. "It wasn't as cold-blooded as that."

"You could have fooled me." Iciness penetrated her voice. "Unlike you, I *do* believe in love, enduring and eternal. And in happy marriages that last a lifetime because love is part of the equation."

"Then I regret saying anything to burst your bubble," he said. "Tell me, though, have *you* ever been 'in love'? I mean really?" Max had put up with enough of Amy Holt's probing. It was time to lob the ball into her court.

CHAPTER FIVE

"THIS isn't about me," Amy said, the color in her cheeks revealing that he'd flustered her, just as he'd aimed to. And Max wasn't about to let her wriggle off his hook.

"You *talk* like an expert." He picked up a sponge, watching her as he made swipes at the table. "Experience vicariously gained, I'd guess."

"One can learn a lot from observation."

"In this arena, observation is a poor second to the real thing. Tell me, Amy, do you have any of your own experiences to bolster those naive theories about love? Has your heart ever beat like a tom-tom over some man? Have you had palpitations the instant a certain guy walked into the room?"

"You're unreal," Amy scolded.

"Me? You're the one living a fantasy. I'll bet hidden under all those bride magazines in your office is a stack of romance novels to feed that fanciful streak of yours. What book were you reading the other night?" He hoped to disconcert her further with the reference to their midnight encounter. If she were human, the recollection would heat her blood just as it did his.

Amy giggled, showing his ploy had failed. "A Dean Koontz thriller. Not exactly a romance."

"Okay, so you win that one. But, Amy..." His eyes were impish again. "Regardless of what you profess to believe, I'll also wager a hundred bucks that you've never been in love, either."

She turned back to the dishwasher and Max assumed she was going to leave this bet unanswered. But then what could she say, he thought smugly, when he was dead right?

Amy finished her work in silence, and once the kitchen was clean, she made a beeline for her suite. At the threshold of the suite, however, she paused, eyeing him levelly. "I'm not like you. Just because I haven't fallen head over heels yet doesn't mean I've lost my faith in it happening someday." Having said that, Amy opened the door and slammed it behind her. *Well, Evans, she told you.* He heard the lock click. *Second message received. She definitely doesn't want your company.*

After a series of channel changes, from an old movie to a World War II documentary to a wildlife special, Amy gave up on television. Her suite felt as confining as a jail cell, yet she wasn't ready for another face-off with Max. She listened. There were no sounds from the rest of the house; apparently he'd taken her hint and gone on to bed. Amy unlocked her door and peeked out. All was silent. The coast was clear.

She ventured into the solarium, her favorite room at Torrence Place. The space had once been a huge screened porch and as a child she'd sat there with her grandparents on hot summer evenings, entranced with their stories of early Houston and the "good old days."

The porch was given priority when she'd begun renovating. Amy had it air-conditioned and enclosed with glass, transforming the area into a multipurpose room. The decorators had outdone themselves, using an abundance of plants to take advantage of the daytime sun, bringing a bit of the outdoors inside.

Darkness had fallen and the room lay in shadows. Comforted by the pleasant stillness, Amy didn't bother with a light. She gazed out the wall of windows, only the faint white outline of the gazebo easily detectable in the night.

"Couldn't sleep?" Max's voice startled her.

She switched on a lamp. "I thought you'd gone upstairs."

"Yeah." He grinned. "Otherwise, you'd still be hiding out behind locked doors. Since you've resurfaced though, let's talk some more."

"I have no interest in hearing more of your disparaging remarks about an emotion I venerate," Amy said, wishing she *was* still hiding out.

"Turnabout's fair play. You want to poke into my affairs, but slam on the brakes as far as your own." Max patted the sofa cushion next to him. "Stay and chat. I promise not to mention your love life again. On my oath as a former Boy Scout." He gave the three-fingered salute before adding, "Since it bothers you so much."

"The Scouts would probably accuse you of sacrilege," Amy said, choosing another chair. "Hiding behind their oath and continuing your needling. If you want me to stay, I suggest you don't talk of anything more controversial than the weather."

"Okay. Think we'll have snow tonight?"

Amy laughed in spite of herself. In all her descriptions of Max, she'd omitted a sense of humor, but clearly he had one. Snow in Houston during the middle of winter was uncommon—any of the white stuff falling in April was as likely as her winning the Texas lottery. "If I say no, you'll probably purchase a snowmaking machine and have my front lawn covered by morning."

"We could build a snowman together."

"Of course. The media could then announce, 'Robin Porter sunbathes in Mexico while Max Evans frolics in the snow on Heights Boulevard.'"

Max's eyes closed as though envisioning the scene. "So no more weather talk. Let's see...safe subject... I know, 'Arrangements by Amy.' You told me how you acquired Torrence Place, but not how it led into the wedding business."

"Strictly by accident," she answered. "I'd been in so many ceremonies—twenty-three stints as a bridesmaid to be exact—that I reasoned I should become a pro."

"Twenty-three's an impressive figure," he said. "But only a bridesmaid—never a bride?"

"Never a bride," she echoed warily. "All I've got to show for those weddings is twenty-three dresses hanging in my closet, each worn only once." Amy shook her head. "There's just something about bridesmaid dresses. They don't recycle well."

Max grinned. "With so many friends, it would have really been tricky to narrow the number of attendants if you'd been my bride."

"It wouldn't have been so hard. Just Steph. We've known each other only a couple of years, but she's become like a sister to me. She..." Amy's voice trailed off. *If you'd been my bride*, he'd said.

"I can see why you have lots of friends," Max interjected. "You're a sensitive woman...nice enough even to put up with me. Do you realize—" he checked his watch "—you haven't suggested I leave for over five hours? You're warming to me, Amy. I can tell."

The ringing telephone broke off Amy's rebuttal. She ran to the kitchen to answer. "It seems I'm serving as your switchboard operator now," she told Max, handing him the cordless receiver. *Warming to him, ha!*

"Hello." Max cupped his hand over the mouthpiece. "Do you mind? It's important. One of my assistants about a hotel deal we're peddling."

"Then I'll give you some privacy. Good night," she said, feeling as if she'd been literally saved by the bell. Max's playful mood and his comment about her being his bride hung in her mind and she didn't know what to make of it all. He was a master at confusing and riling her, only this time she was simply confused.

She slept in Saturday morning. Amazingly, her concerns over the potential damage to "Arrangements by Amy" hadn't followed her to bed. Even having Max upstairs hadn't bothered her. Quite the contrary, she'd felt secure knowing there was a man in the house. *Quit being dumb*, she chided. *Don't get used to this, because it's going to end as soon as you can manage it.*

She was having her first cup of coffee when the doorbell rang. Max must have already been on his way downstairs. He was opening the door as she entered the foyer.

"Have you seen this?" Without any word of greeting, Jenna shoved a newspaper in his hand. She rested a palm at his waist, hovering close while Max scanned the article

From three feet away, Amy could tell the picture was of Robin, in a bikini. The accompanying headline read: "Don't Cry For Me, Max Evans."

"Damn!" Max said. Then he, Jenna and the newspaper disappeared upstairs, Jenna's arms entwined with one of Max's. Amy went out to retrieve her own morning paper and carried it with her into the kitchen.

The publicity had gone from bad to worse. Torrence Place was once again mentioned in the article, rein-forcing the implication that the wedding site was somehow responsible for what had transpired. If the people yet to be married here weren't already spooked, then this latest article ought to do it.

Tossing the paper aside, Amy resolved to get to work She'd barely sat down at her desk when the phone started ringing. The first calls were from sympathetic girl-friends, their encouragement quickly dashed by two more cancellations. Exasperated and seeking a physical outlet,

Amy headed to the kitchen. She'd clean cabinets or something, anything to control her troubled mind.

The coffee carafe and some pastries were missing. Max must have come down and carried them to his room. Jenna was still up there with him, making Amy wonder anew what was going on between the two of them. "It doesn't take half the morning to discuss a newspaper article," she said aloud. Could it be that the article was long forgotten and they'd digressed to more intimate discussions? Amy tried to comfort herself with that notion. If Max was taking a liking to Jenna, then maybe he would pursue her on out the door. But the idea didn't make Amy feel any better.

She heard Max and his guest stirring just as the phone summoned her again. It was Marie Howard calling off her Christmas wedding. Amy could tell from her flimsy excuse that Marie was reacting to the current Torrence Place notoriety.

"It's too bad the date didn't work out," Amy said, "but if you decide on another, I can still reschedule you in the next few days. Yes. Yes. I see . . ." Amy switched off the cordless phone and dropped it in her apron pocket as she sank into a chair. "A pox on you," she muttered aloud, then glanced up to see Max watching her from the doorway.

"Trouble?"

She nodded.

"Because of me?"

"She blamed it on her job—a conflicting conference."

"And you don't buy that?"

"No. Christmas isn't a popular season for company conferences. Then she balked when I suggested picking another date."

He came over and joined Amy at the kitchen table. "I'm sorry. I'll make—"

"It's not your problem," Amy interrupted. "I'll handle it myself. I don't need your sympathy or your help. Go entertain your little friend."

"You mean Jenna?"

"Who else?" It wasn't like Amy to be so testy, but she simply couldn't control her tongue. She was being buffeted from all sides.

"Jenna left. She just came over to warn me about the article, then we talked a bit." He smiled. "She's really a nice person. Why does her coming here annoy you so?"

"Don't be silly. She doesn't annoy me at all." Amy rose from her chair. "If you'll excuse me, I have work stacked up in my office."

"Okay," he said agreeably. "By the way, Jenna brought my laptop and cellular phone over. Now I can conduct a bit of business and not interfere with yours." He trotted upstairs, leaving a shamefaced Amy standing alone.

She hadn't meant to be so crabby and unreasonable about her telephone, nor to behave so shrewishly about Jenna. Max must think her a nut case. And rightly so. Since the moment he'd become a part of her existence, she'd become erratic and irrational.

Max's footfalls had no sooner hit the top of the stairs before she heard him retracing his steps. "Listen," he said to her, grabbing Amy and massaging her shoulders, "I'm bored stiff."

Amy tried to shrug free—his touches were occurring too frequently—but he held on. "I'm sorry the entertainment at Torrence Place isn't more scintillating," she snapped. "Why don't I invite a squad of comedians to help you while away the hours? Or would you prefer the 'Baywatch' women or the Dallas Cowboys cheerleaders?"

Max ignored the jabs. "I'd rather while the hours away with you."

"I'm busy." She hadn't expected Max to use the opportunity to fold her into his arms. Amy braced her hands against his chest. "Please leave me alone," she pleaded.

"Only if you agree to take me for a drive...a long one." Max loosened his hold and stepped back to lean against the table, giving her space to make a decision. "I'm getting positively claustrophobic hunkered down alone in the Hearts and Flowers. It's not doing a lot for my manly image, either. Can you see the write-up—'Missing groom Max Evans finally discovered hiding among the eyelet pillows and the potpourri.' Worse than that snow scene you conjured up."

Amy patted his shoulder. "*Poor baby.*"

"That's right. Poor me. Have you no mercy for a lonely man?"

"Why didn't you have Jenna rescue you?"

"Couldn't. She was expected at her hair salon."

"The way the woman was fawning over you, I'm certain she'd have broken the appointment if you'd only crooked your little finger."

"But I didn't."

Was Max indicating he hadn't wanted to be with Jenna, that he preferred her company instead? Amy began to wonder if she'd misinterpreted Max's interest in his early morning visitor. But Jenna or no Jenna, all logic said an outing with Max could lead to complications. She'd have to say no.

Logic short-circuited by a persuasive Max, thirty minutes later they were in her car on the way to Galveston Island, fifty-odd miles from Houston. "Are you sure we should be doing this?" Amy asked belatedly, already knowing the answer. "What if someone recognizes you?"

"We'll avoid the Strand and lunch somewhere other than Guido's. Just two anonymous tourists, out for a day of sun and surf. If anyone's seriously searching, they won't expect me to be down here."

Amy wasn't so confident, but it had been ages since she'd had a non-work-related outing and the smell of salt air as they drove over the causeway separating the mainland from Galveston pleasantly assaulted her senses. With Max in the house, her routine had been shot to pieces anyway, so she might as well enjoy the day.

After purchasing a take-out lunch of shrimp and French fries, they located an uncrowded stretch of beach which offered relative privacy. They'd finished the meal when a young family drove up and settled nearby. The parents were busy erecting a canopy when a small boy came over.

"Wanna play?" he asked Max, swinging a Frisbee in front of him.

"Yeah," Max answered, rising and dusting sand off his jeans. "As soon as I feed the birds the rest of our lunch. Why don't you help me?"

The child eagerly agreed and Amy watched the two indulge a flock of gulls brazenly begging for a handout. With the leftovers gone and the gulls seeking greener pastures, Max gently sailed the bright red disk for the giggling boy to chase. Once the canopy was up, the boy's father came over and spoke to Max. "Thanks. I'll relieve you now."

"I enjoyed it," Max said, tousling the boy's hair. He rejoined Amy. "Need me to dust you off?" he teased, as she rose to her feet.

"No, thank you. By the way, you're good with children."

"Don't sound so surprised. I really like kids. Now let's go ride the ferry." Max sounded almost like a youngster himself.

They drove a few miles, then lined up behind a group of cars waiting to take the short ferry ride between Galveston and Port Bolivar. It was a trip Amy hadn't made in ages, but she still remembered the thrill of standing at the rail, the wind in her hair, her father's arms enclosing her as they searched the water for sea creatures.

Once Amy's car was parked on board, Max helped her out. They took a place by the rail and his arms steadied her, just as her father's once had. The experience was as thrilling as in her youth, albeit in an entirely different way.

"Look." Max pointed toward the flock of scavenger gulls following the craft. One of the greedy birds had bravely perched on a passenger's shoulder, gingerly accepting treats from the stranger. Feeling rather daring herself, Amy relaxed against Max and his arms wrapped around her, holding her close.

At sundown, they had supper at an out-of-the-way seafood restaurant. "It's been a fine day," he said, and she nodded. They had indulged themselves in people watching, seen a few sights, discussed favorite books and new movies. As if by mutual consent, there'd been no mention of Max's wedding or Torrence Place or their respective love lives. Amy hadn't wanted to interrupt the serenity of the day, and he'd seemed to agree.

She'd been exposed to a new side of Max, tender, fun-loving. Although she'd been attracted to him from the beginning, Amy had managed to fight his appeal by amplifying his negative qualities. After today, recalling the negatives was going to be more difficult.

"Let's take a walk on the beach before starting back to Houston," he suggested. They parked the car in a sandy cove and Max removed his shoes and socks and rolled up his pant legs. Amy shed her sandals and they strolled at the edge of the water, dodging waves and tiny sand crabs. When he took her hand, Amy didn't object.

"Thank you for today," he said, cradling her cheek with his other hand. It meant..." His eyes intensified to a deeper violet as they locked with hers, their unspoken message telling Amy that he wanted more than the touch, that he wanted to bring his lips to hers. She felt herself swaying toward him and the light press of his mouth on hers ignited her senses. She wanted him to pull her closer, to... It would feel so good, so right...wrong! Amy wrenched away so abruptly that she stumbled backward, almost falling.

"Let me help." He reached for her.

"No, please," she said, her voice shaky as she recovered her balance. "Really, I'm fine," she insisted, gazing up at the sky, trying to lower her out-of-control pulse rate. "Look, there's a full moon tonight," she said, attempting to distract Max's attention with the mundane.

"All the better to see you with, my dear," he growled. "You're very beautiful, you know." He reached for her again.

Amy eluded him and started toward the car. "It's late, time to hasten to Grandmother's house." *And to be wary of Big Bad Wolves*.

The drive back was strained, the scene on the beach undermining the earlier camaraderie. The clock was striking ten when they arrived home. Amy hurried to check her messages—none—and Max, making himself at home, plopped onto her couch and clicked on the television to watch the evening news. She'd no sooner joined him in front of the set than a shot of Torrence

Place came on the screen. *This day was fast going down the drain*. Amy flinched, holding her breath at what was to come.

"Houston is agog with the ongoing rumors about real estate developer Max Evans and socialite Robin Porter." The picture switched to a head shot of one of the evening anchors. "First, the pair's last-minute halt of their wedding. Now Ms. Porter has surfaced, vacationing on a sunny Cancún beach with an unnamed male. Although neither the Porter nor Evans families will officially comment, an anonymous source says it was Ms. Porter who spurned the millionaire bachelor. Max Evans is in seclusion."

"'Spurned'? 'Seclusion'? He's making it sound like Robin dumped me and I'm off somewhere licking my wounds."

"Aren't you? I kept telling you to issue a statement, and you kept putting me off. At least you could have had your say then."

"Believe it or not, I was trying to behave like a gentleman. It never dawned on me that she'd take this route."

"Well, phone someone and clear it up."

"It's a little late for that, don't you think? Any kind of news release would just seem like face-saving on my part. I'd hoped for Robin to be more discreet."

What could Amy say to assuage the blow? She had to give him credit for taking the high road, trying to keep the details private. Unfortunately for him, he was no longer in control of Robin Porter, and it appeared as if she was feeding her own version to the media. "I'm sorry," Amy soothed.

"I don't want sympathy. I want—"

"What? Revenge?"

"I didn't say that."

"It's what you were thinking, though, wasn't it?"

"Maybe...for a second." He shook his head and grinned. "How do you suggest I do it? Scribble her phone number on rest room walls? Cancel her charge accounts? Announce that she's had a tummy tuck?" He started snickering and before long was laughing outright.

"Has she?" Amy was giggling now also, her business worries and the confusing feelings over Max's lovemaking pushed to the recesses of her mind.

"No, but people would believe it anyway."

"You wouldn't do any of those things—would you?"

"No, I'm not so vindictive. But they're fun to contemplate." He chuckled again.

His merriment was infectious and Amy laughed along. Max traced his knuckles across her cheekbones, a repeat gesture she rather liked. "Thanks for helping me put things in perspective. You're good for me, Amy Holt." He stood up, then grimaced. "I must smell like a sea bass. Give me time for a shower and we'll have a nightcap." Amy was prepared to tell him she was too tired, but before she could beg off, Max was already gone.

Well, she hadn't really wanted the evening to end, Amy admitted as she took a fast bath and changed into jeans and a sleeveless chambray shirt. She considered a bathrobe instead, but decided it was safer to be fully dressed. She didn't want to provide any more inadvertent peep shows or give Max grounds for thinking she was inviting another of his kisses—or more than kisses.

When she returned to the solarium, Max was already there, pulling the cork on a bottle of champagne. On seeing her, the serious expression on his face conflicted with the open admiration in his eyes.

"I need to ask you something, Amy, and I'd like an honest answer."

His tone of voice made her stiffen. Amy sank into a wicker rocking chair. "Just when have I been dishonest?" she hedged.

"On this particular issue, I suspect you've been less than candid. Tell me, how bad are your finances?"

"That subject is not open for discussion," she said.

"Really rough, hmm?"

"I didn't say that. Why do you want to know anyway?"

"Because I realize I've inadvertently harmed your business. Unfavorable publicity, cancellations..."

She waved her hand in a dismissive gesture. "That's the way it goes in the wedding game. Cancellations happen."

"How often do you have two in two days?"

"Well, I..." He didn't realize there were actually four. She waved her hand again. "As I said earlier, it's not your problem, so don't lose any sleep over it. I'll recover." *Big talk. Empty talk.*

"I'm sure you will. But there's got to be a way I can rectify my role in your troubles."

Past conduct told Amy that Max would unhesitatingly provide monetary recompense if she so much as blinked. The possibility was too distasteful. "I'd prefer you to forget it. After all, I'm a certified adult, capable of digging my own way out."

"I'd still like to help." He filled crystal flutes with the bubbly and handed her one. "Cheers."

Amy responded with a tap of her glass against his. "It hardly seems an occasion for celebrating," she added, wondering what he was up to.

"Oh, you never can tell," he said, sitting down across from her. "Maybe if we put our heads together, we'll come up with an occasion." All of a sudden he was smiling as though he'd stumbled onto a cure for the ozone depletion.

Defying a host of internal warnings, Amy allowed her spirits to brighten at the smile. Max always struck her as the handsomest man she'd ever seen, but with those worry lines gone and— She must stop this. Max Evans was like a muscle pull... a wrong move and you discover nerves you didn't know you'd had before. There was no reason to believe he'd ever be anything but problematic. She should be suspicious about why he was so darn pleased with himself right now, not starry-eyed over his good looks.

They sat there for a long while, sipping the pale liquid, neither speaking. Amy was too busy ruing her reactions to Max and Max seemed to be plotting something. Something troublesome, most likely.

"I'm hungry," he finally said, standing up.

Amy gave an exaggerated sigh. "Here I was wondering what evil you were planning and all you're thinking about is your stomach."

"I'd be happy to switch to something evil if you prefer." His eyebrows raised in mock anticipation.

"Oh, no, food's just fine. What do you want me to fix?"

"Allow me," Max insisted, disappearing into the kitchen. She heard cabinets and the refrigerator opening and closing, then Max returned with a tray of fruit, cheese and crackers.

"This domestic turn might harm your stature as a man-about-town." She was striving for a caustic tone, but the words sounded more complimentary than abrasive.

"This old dog has lots of tricks," he answered, "but I'm always ready to learn a few more. Want to tutor me?"

"I'm not about to touch that one."

"I guarantee I'd be an apt pupil. Maybe even teacher's pet."

Amy shook her head determinedly, drawing a smile from him.

Max refilled their glasses with champagne, then placed the bottle in a wine cooler. Leaving the innuendos behind, he took on the role of host, entertaining her with witty anecdotes and tales from his world.

His good cheer and the champagne made Amy forget their mutual woes for a few hours, but it was late and she knew it would be wise to bring closure to this evening while the mood was still light.

She rose and carried the tray to the kitchen, Max following her. As she rinsed the dishes, he came up behind her and placed his hands on both sides of the counter, trapping her. "I have an idea," he murmured, nuzzling her neck.

She shut off the faucet and turned around, her damp hands making a pattern on Max's cotton shirt as she attempted to break free. He refused to cede any ground and mere inches separated their bodies. Amy could feel his breath as he spoke.

"Remember when we were talking about a scandal to counter the wedding stories?"

Amy nodded. "Has there been one?"

"Not yet."

"Then what? Have you decided to hire some celebrity to create a sensation?"

"No, nothing that nefarious. But the reputation of Torrence Place has been sullied and I've thought of a way to blunt any further harm." He was stroking her bare arms, clearly pleased about the goose bumps his touches triggered.

"I told you not to worry about Torrence Place," she said, her voice husky in reaction to the prolonged closeness.

"I can't help it. I'm too distressed about you."

"Are you positive your distress doesn't center on something closer to home—like Max Evans's reputation?" She suspected that tonight's newscast was his main concern. It had been mostly about him and Robin, not Torrence Place, which had gotten just a brief mention. Amy shoved against Max again, but he was as immovable as before.

"I think my psyche can withstand a little embarrassment," he said. "But that's irrelevant. We'd both benefit from my idea."

Amy looked skeptical. "And your idea *is*?"

"It's very spontaneous, very romantic. Right up your alley."

Somehow she doubted that. In the time she'd known Max Evans, she wouldn't classify a thing he'd done as genuinely spontaneous and he'd been about as romantic as an old sock. *Until today*. "And what did you have in mind?"

"Something so simple, it's brilliant. We could elope."

CHAPTER SIX

AMY was too shocked to respond, or even to move. She stood there, frozen between Max and the counter, gaping up at him.

"Hang on before you say anything," he ordered. "I'll send our pilot to ready the family jet and have my travel agent reserve a suite at one of those hotels along the strip. We can be in Las Vegas in a couple of hours."

She pushed out of his arms and crossed the kitchen, attempting to gain some protective yardage. The man couldn't be serious. Amy leaned against the doorjamb, watching him and wondering whether she should laugh or call the loony bin patrol.

"Well, what do you think?" Max seemed determined to keep up the pretense. He moved closer, backing Amy into the solarium. When she sat down on the wicker couch, he joined her, crossing one denim-clad leg atop the other and resting an arm on the chintz cushions behind her. "Will you marry me?" Max asked tenderly, his hand slipping onto her shoulder to pull her closer.

The warmth of his touch radiated through her and his skin sent off the aroma of now-familiar after-shave. Inviting even more sensory overload, she made the mistake of glancing into those blue eyes. *Yes*, a breathless voice almost agreed.

Then Amy caught herself. So they'd spent a few pleasant hours together. She couldn't let that cloud her brain. Two days ago Max was waiting to wed Robin and, disclaimers aside, Amy wasn't certain he wasn't still harboring feelings for the woman. Just because he'd said he didn't believe in love didn't mean all caring for Robin was obliterated.

Amy didn't want a rebound husband. And, even if that stumbling block didn't exist, there were a dozen others. Without considering any of those impediments, a union between her and Max was beyond the pale. Their brief acquaintance hardly measured up as friendship, much less a basis for escalating that relationship to marriage. *To think I'm even having this debate with myself. Now who's ready for the loony bin?*

Mockingly she pressed a palm to Max's forehead. "No fever, so I suppose we'll have to chalk this lapse up to the champagne. Just in case it's not the champagne, however, let's get something straight right now. I have no intention of participating in this goofy escapade you've dreamed up."

"I realize I've surprised you, but you shouldn't dismiss my proposal out of hand." Max hadn't really expected her to agree, and was puzzled by his disappointment. Disappointment was an unfamiliar emotion for him. He hadn't felt any regret about Robin. No, he distinctly remembered his immediate reaction to that—relief. Soul-cleansing relief. So why did he feel let down now?

Max pressed the veins of his temple. Sure Amy was pretty, with a soft full mouth and brown velvet eyes you could lose yourself in. A majority of the women he knew had beautiful features. Sure she was intelligent and feisty and fun to be with. So were a lot of the women in his life. Nothing explained his confusion or his desire to crush his lips to hers and kiss away all her hesitation...

Rising from the couch, Amy stood to face Max, her arms crossed defensively. "It boggles my mind we're having this discussion. I know you're joking, but it isn't funny."

"Some things I don't joke about. Proposing marriage is one of those things. Marry me, Amy."

"Why? Is there some reason you *need* a wife?"

"What makes you think that?"

"What else could have induced such an impetuous proposition? I mean, you just got 'disengaged' and now you're ready to try again. I can't help wondering why me and why the big hurry?"

"Why you?" Max rose to his feet and faced her, cupping her chin in his hand. "Because you're smart and beautiful. Any man would be proud to have you as his wife."

Why the hurry? she'd also asked. Max wasn't sure he understood himself, except to explain when he made up his mind to do something, he acted—unless logic told him to take it slow. Right now, logic be damned. "I can't see any reason for waiting. Just the opposite. The sooner we get it over with, the sooner our lives will return to normal." Max knew he'd said the wrong thing the instant the words were out of his mouth.

"You make the prospect sound as appealing as a tax audit. The only prayer I have of my life returning to normal is to get *you* out of it." Amy looked as though she was either going to burst into tears or throw a handy lamp his way. He guessed he'd have to risk lamps or tears or both.

"If you're through stomping all over my ego, how about reconsidering your answer," he said. "You as much as admitted earlier that you've never been in love—and neither have I. So we're perfect for each other. I'm getting long in the tooth for a blushing bridegroom and pretty soon you're going to be branded an old maid." He hoped the teasing would help override his blunder of a minute ago. "Do you want that to happen?"

"Women's concern about spinsterhood went out with the Ford Edsel. About the time women's liberation came in. Or hadn't you heard?" She didn't sound placated.

"Women still want to get married. No matter how liberated."

"And men—"

Max's quick kiss stopped the riposte in midsentence. "Men, too. Don't forget Torrence Place and your business," he added, reminding both himself and Amy what his proposal had really been about. He wanted to make amends and this was the best way to do it. "Motive enough for us to speed to the altar. Shall I alert the pilot?"

"A Las Vegas wedding," Amy said, moving toward the windows. "I can see it all now." She gestured expansively. "A garish neon-lit chapel. The two of us dressed in our jeans surrounded by plastic flowers and a group—a chorus even—of fake Elvises. Just the kind of wedding I've always dreamed of." She slumped down in an armchair, resting her neck against the cushion and shooting him an insolent glare.

"It doesn't have to be that way." He grinned. Amy had a cute tendency to overdramatize. "Unless you're in such a rush to be Mrs. Max Evans that you can't wait, you can change to a dress before we leave. And no plastic posies, I'll have a florist provide all the real ones you want—roses, carnations, gardenias, orchids. So, again, what do you say?"

"What do I say?" Amy shook her head vigorously. "In plain language, no way. A stupid stunt like that is just what I don't need. Do you really think something this harebrained would solve my problems?"

"Maybe not all of them, but—"

"Forget it. I don't want to elope and I'm not going to listen to another word of this inane conversation." Childishly, Amy covered her ears.

Max tugged her hands down. "An engagement, then?"

"You're certifiably crazy!"

His patience was waning. He'd tried every tactic he knew to make her agree. Why did the woman have to be so pigheaded? "No, not crazy, practical," he growled, "trying to figure some way out of this mess."

"Practical!" *That word again.* Amy'd had her fill of it. "'Practical' should be your motto. Well, I'm sorry, but I don't want practicality—I want passion!"

The corners of his mouth betrayed a slight twitch. "I promise I can be very passionate in the appropriate setting." The sensuous look he gave her sparked Amy's imagination, raising her temperature to tropical proportions.

Dummy, you walked right into that. No doubt he could deliver on the promise. "I'm sure," she said, fighting off that ever-betraying blush. "The only problem," she added with a trace of bitterness, "is that it doesn't matter who your partner is. Female appears to be the only criterion." She recalled that she was the third woman in Max's life in about as many days.

"Let me tell you something, Max Evans. I don't think of marriage as a licensed roll in the hay and I don't think just *anyone* will do. When I say yes, it will be because I love the man to distraction—and because he feels the same way about me—and me alone." *Love, a word Max had judiciously avoided in his spur-of-the-moment proposal.* "Until then, I'll handle my own problems. I don't need any help from you to extricate myself from this 'mess.'"

"Maybe I need your help."

"Then you're out of luck. If you're so eager to tie the knot, I suggest you search elsewhere for a bride. Surely you can find someone who'll have you. Or has Jenna already turned you down, too?" Amy felt a pang of conscience at her thoughtless remarks, but immediately forgave herself. Max'd brought all this down on his own head. Choosing Robin was shortsighted in the first place and now he was trying to salvage his self-esteem with another thinly disguised marriage of convenience. How dare he treat something as holy as marriage so lightly?

"Okay, we'll drop the idea for now," Max conceded. "Maybe tomorrow you can discuss it more rationally."

"Me? I'm not the one being irrational. Let's clear something up—we're not discussing anything tomorrow. I want you out of my house—preferably right now."

"Are we riding that dead horse again?" He patted a hand over his mouth, feigning a yawn. "I'm not leaving."

"We'll see about that," she threatened lamely as she stormed off to her suite.

Tomorrow. Steph and Jay are back from their trip. As soon as they're up... Oh, it was useless and Amy knew it. Max'd insisted on putting down a hefty deposit for his stay, thereby preventing any legal recourse. She'd simply have to persevere until he became too bored to stick around any longer. She couldn't see Steph's husband trying to throw him out. For one thing, Max was half a foot taller and at least thirty pounds heavier. For another, Jay was preparing to become a surgeon. He wouldn't risk injuring his hands in a stupid brawl, something that just might result if Max was pushed into defending himself.

She pulled a pair of pajamas from her antique armoire. *Elope.* Of all the outlandish... The absurd part of it was the way her heart actually skipped a beat when he'd suggested it. If she gave vent to her fantasies, Amy could picture herself hopping on that jet with Max. She could close her eyes and envision that outrageous wedding—right down to the Elvis impersonators.

What was wrong with her? It was as if some alien presence had subverted her thought processes. With Max on the scene, nothing was close to ordinary. She had to be free of him—her emotional well-being depended on it.

An aroma of coffee awakened her the next morning. "Thank you, Stephie," Amy mumbled as she slowly drew back the covers. The digital clock showed nine. Time to get busy. Quickly showering and dressing—just in case her unwanted guest was up and about—she went to the kitchen.

"Good morning, Miss Slugabed," Stephanie chirped. She was taking a stack of napkins from the linen closet. "We figured the coffee would rouse you."

We? As Amy started to phrase the question aloud, Max entered with the Sunday paper in hand. "I retrieved this from the front lawn. Thought I'd check the latest fallout."

"More bad news is just what I need," Amy grumbled, pouring herself a cup of coffee. She already had enough worries on her plate without scouring the papers for more, her *foremost* worry being the possibility of Max bringing up that silly proposal in front of Stephanie. Without a doubt Steph would go right along with him, think it a wonderful idea. Amy could see that Max had made an ally of her friend and she was in no mood to battle both of them. Besides, today belonged to Ralph and Eva and she didn't want any negative forces intruding.

Normally, Amy would have hunched over the kitchen table sipping her coffee till she completely awakened. Now she didn't know what to do. It didn't seem a good idea to leave Max and Steph alone, but she didn't feel comfortable staying around them, either. As a compromise, Amy stayed, but occupied herself by thumbing through her recipe box. She had only a few hours to prepare the chicken and wild rice casserole for Ralph and Eva's luncheon, so she might as well get started.

Max removed the newspaper from its plastic bag and leafed through the sections. Stephanie flitted about, treating the man as if he were a foreign potentate, serving him a platter of miniature muffins with crocks of flavored butter and freshening his coffee every time he set his cup down.

"Well, we're still in the news," Max announced. He brought a folded section over to Amy, holding it while she scanned the article. "Countermeasures are called for."

"Looks to me as though the hubbub is subsiding. At least it's off the front page." Amy waved the paper away, her eyes avoiding Max's. She wasn't about to subject herself to any pressure from him or provide an opportunity for more conversation on their marrying.

"See, I told you everything would be okay," the everoptimistic Steph chimed in, oblivious to the high-voltage current running between Amy and Max.

"You're right, Steph, everything's going to be fine." Amy turned to Max. "Now, if you'll excuse us, Mr. Evans, we need to concentrate on work."

She thought he was going to argue, but instead Max refilled his coffee and picked up the newspaper. "Mind if I borrow this?"

He was barely out of the room when Stephanie started in. "What's the deal? You could have knocked me over with a hummingbird feather when I came upon Max in the kitchen this morning, acting like he's taken up permanent residence. Obviously you've gotten to know each other quite well in my absence," she said. Her face showed undisguised hopefulness. "What's he doing here? And what's going on between you? Tell me what I've missed."

"Hiding out from the press, nothing going on and what you've missed is four cancellations. Gail Weinberg, Patti Brinks, Veronica Pineda and Marie Howard bailed out while you were gone."

"Oh, no." Steph squeezed Amy's hand sympathetically.

"And you should see the horrid picture of Torrence Place they've been running."

Stephanie grimaced. "All of this is because of Max's bombed-out wedding?"

"It appears to be. Haven't you been reading the papers or listening to the news?"

Stephanie wriggled her eyebrows suggestively in response. Of course she hadn't, Amy remembered. She and Jay probably never left their motel room. "It's been a circus with the press, and the repercussions are even worse than I feared. The cancellations have come in so fast, my head is spinning."

"Really, Amy. I'm so sorry. But what about Max? Can't he do something?"

"Oh, right. Like he's some sort of wizard who can fix everything. What could he do? Whip out that checkbook of his?" She had no intention of sharing Max's elopement idea with Stephanie. That remedy wasn't worth another second of her thoughts, or the interminable discussion that would follow if she did mention it.

"But he's a wheeler-dealer," Stephanie said. "He should understand that money is only part of the problem."

"I'm not sure he does. And even if he did, I don't see any way he could help with reestablishing a positive image of Torrence Place. No, this is my problem and I've got to figure out the solution myself." *And marrying Max Evans definitely isn't it.*

That afternoon's wedding was one of her best, Amy decided. Eva and Ralph surrounded by children, grandchildren and several friends from the retirement home. Perhaps it was the sincerity of the couple that made the difference, but Amy had that familiar feel-good tingle that came with launching a new union. It was like a tonic after Thursday's upheaval.

She did experience a bit of apprehension when Max joined the wedding party. However, he was everything Amy thought he wouldn't be—ingratiating, and useful. He served punch and coffee, assisted in clearing the luncheon table and folded the chairs away. The extra pair of hands contributed to a smooth operation and Amy couldn't help but be appreciative.

By the end of the afternoon, one would have guessed Max to be a member of the family, especially when he made the gracious gesture of arranging for Eva and Ralph to have that honeymoon in Maui he'd planned for himself. It galled Amy to admit that Max was being— to borrow a Mary Poppins turn of phrase—practically perfect in every way.

By sundown, the guests had left, then Stephanie. Amy and Max had finished an early supper and were seated at a table in the solarium winding down with a glass of iced tea.

"Today was fun," he said. "I can see why you like your work. It must be very gratifying."

"Generally," she admitted.

"Except when weddings blow up in your face, like mine did, hmm?"

"Yes," Amy answered, not wanting to carry the conversation further. It was still too painful for her and she was unable to deal with her perplexing feelings about what had happened since then.

Amy expected Max to belabor last night's proposal, but he didn't. She wasn't sure whether he was biding his time before starting in again or if he'd reconsidered his rash offer and changed his mind. That would be more plausible. The notion bothered Amy. Could a pattern be showing up? Did Max like flirting with the idea of marriage but start waffling when it came to the actual commitment? Maybe there were others besides Lucy Walsh and Robin Porter who'd misunderstood his true intentions.

Now that Amy could relax, inexplicably she felt miffed that he'd given up on her so readily. She should be happy with some simple conversation and a calm evening. She didn't need amorous advances or half-baked strategies to ease her struggles.

"Doesn't it get tiresome?" His query broke into her jumbled reverie and tempered her sulky mood.

"Huh?...Oh, the business. No, I like what I do," she said. "I savor every wedding." She would keep it impersonal and not single his out as the obvious exception.

"Don't they all begin to seem the same?"

Amy shook her head. "Not to me. The people make the difference. I work at ensuring that each affair is individualized, not an assembly-line product. Besides, there are some that are really unusual."

"Example?"

Amy peaked her fingers as she thought. "There was one at the surf's edge in Galveston, with all the guests ankle-deep in the water. Then another at a Randall's. The aisle ran right through the produce section—"

"A grocery store ceremony? And you accuse me of being unromantic. What was your favorite one? Which storybook affair?"

"What makes you think that's what it'd take to be my favorite?" Amy asked, relieved he hadn't seized on her mention of Galveston to make some reference to that embrace on the beach, or to start in again about eloping.

"Because I know you, Amy, my love."

She paid no attention to the endearment. "I've lots of favorites. But one a couple of years ago at the Indian Temple sticks in my mind. The bride wore a red silk sari. It was truly lovely."

Amy gave thanks that they were still talking about other people's weddings. Apparently, Max wasn't going to introduce the elopement discussion again. Her declaration that she'd handle her difficulties on her own must have gotten through. Astonishing, in light of how seldomly he heeded anything she said.

She squeezed a lemon wedge into the tea and felt better. Her business woes wouldn't go away, but right now she didn't have to think about them. And for once, it seemed as though Max agreed.

She traced a heart into the cloud of moisture on her glass. "Did you know," she continued, "that in a Hindu household, a daughter symbolizes the goddess of wealth? So when a daughter is given to her groom, her parents are in effect offering the prime wealth of the household. Isn't that sweet?"

"I think you're sweet, Amy Holt." Max leaned over and kissed her on the cheek—a light, friendly sort of kiss, but nevertheless disturbing, considering all that had transpired yesterday. Before she had a chance to protest, he slid back to his end of the couch.

"You'd think a wedding was the last place in the world I'd choose to be, but I enjoyed today." He reached over and took her hand. "And I'm longing to attend another ceremony. Soon."

So he hadn't abandoned the subject after all. Bridging her defenses with small talk, then pouncing was hardly fair play. "I thought we'd settled that." She tried to pull free of his grip, but Max held fast and Amy surrendered to having her hand held. Better that than a wrestling match. She didn't see wrestling with Max as a wise thing to do.

"Why haven't you entertained the prospect of marriage before?" His eyes twinkled. "Before me, I mean."

"How do you know I haven't?"

"I asked Stephanie."

She glared at him. "So you've started snooping on me behind my back."

"Only because you refused to talk. According to her, there've been no fiancés and no significant boyfriends."

"Remind me to fire Stephanie."

"If you do, I'll give her a job. So tell me—why?"

"Why *hadn't* you?" Amy retorted. "Before Robin, that is."

"Could be I've tried, as you said. Maybe all the women walk out on me at the last minute."

She rolled her eyes. "On that note, I think I'll walk, too. Goodnight." She rose from her chair.

"Okay, straight answer. Just stay and hear me out. I guess I never realized how nice a relationship could be, how important it is to have someone really special in your life."

For an instant Amy dared to hope Max had been converted, that the afternoon with Ralph and Eva had made him see the wonder of love. Then common sense surfaced. This was Max Evans she was talking to, a man who admittedly didn't know the first thing about the subject. "I suppose you saw the light about the time you discovered Robin had taken to the Cancún beaches with another man."

"No. It started before that."

"Oh?"

"Yes." He stood and took both her hands in his. "I remember exactly when the realization began...it started the day I met you."

CHAPTER SEVEN

THE warm glow in Max's eyes held Amy tighter than a shackle and should have been a prelude to an embrace. But it wasn't. Instead, his words hung between them, thick as a heavy fog. She could see the glow fade as his pronouncement brought no response.

Finally she stammered, "Wha...what are you saying, Max?" If the impossible had happened and he had fallen in love with her, Amy needed to hear the words.

"I'm saying you're very dear to me and that I intend to marry you." He gave her a perfunctory, unsatisfying peck on the forehead. "But you obviously aren't ready to say 'yes.' Okay, then, I'll simply have to be patient." He looped an arm around her and walked her out of the room, to the door of her suite. "As I recall, you have an early meeting tomorrow. So off to bed, sweetheart," he said in his best Bogart voice.

Such a narrow escape from Max's compelling presence and one which Amy accepted gladly. Once she was alone, however, she regretted her inaction. She had so many questions, questions which were now churning inside her.

Max had said she was "very dear" to him. What precisely did that mean? His sisters and his dog—if he had one—were probably very dear to him, too. According to Max's own statement, he'd never experienced love. Was he trying to tell her that had changed? Though dubious, Amy couldn't resist hoping that perhaps...

Her appointment calendar called for a morning inspection of a new interdenominational chapel near Rice

University. Amy was relieved Max was not up when she ventured out; she needed more time to sort out what was happening between them. Now she'd have the entire trip to mull over his startling disclosures and decide what she wanted to say when she saw him again.

On the drive to the chapel and home, Amy reflected and fretted, fretted and reflected. One part of her, that foolishly susceptible part, craved hearing more of Max's endearments. Then the cautious Amy would take over to advise her that she might be overreacting to a bit of impromptu sweet talk, warning that, in all likelihood, she was little more than a brief diversion for a man in crisis. A child could see they were as different as catfish and caviar. The Max Evanses of this world didn't fall in love with the Amy Holts. Did they...?

The rude blast of a horn from the car behind jolted her to the present. The light was green. She needed to get home and talk to Max.

Amy dashed into the house—not ready to agree to the elopement, but anxious to hear him out. She almost stumbled on a set of suitcases piled by the front door. Max was leaning over the dining room table writing out a check.

"What's going on?" she asked, trying to mask her confusion and disappointment.

He pulled a suit jacket off the back of a chair, slinging it over his shoulder. "An emergency in Dallas. A deal I've been putting together for more than a year is about to fall apart, one of the investors trying to bail out. I've got to go up there and convince him otherwise."

"What about the press?"

"I'd have to face the music eventually."

"But it's only been a few days. Are you certain—"

Max laughed. "Is this Amy Holt I'm hearing? What a turnabout. All those harangues to get me to go away and now when I'm leaving, you're objecting. Sounds as though you'll miss me."

"In your dreams," Amy retorted, tamping down her hurt. If she hadn't happened home when she did, Max would have been long gone with only a personal check as a reminder he'd even been here. What a sap she'd been, spending all morning speculating about a potential future with him. There would be no future.

"Oh, you'll be in my dreams, all right, pretty Amy," he shot back. The doorbell pealed. "There's my driver." He tore off the check and handed it to her. "For any expenses my deposit didn't cover."

When she refused to take it, Max shrugged and dropped the check on the table. "While I'm in Dallas you can do more thinking about Las Vegas. I'll call when I get home." The bell sounded again and Max pulled her to him for a quick, but thorough kiss. Then he rushed out.

Sprawled on the seat of his company limousine, an open briefcase beside him, Max couldn't shake the feeling he'd made a strategical error by leaving so abruptly. It troubled him. Yet he'd had little choice. The situation in Dallas needed his immediate personal attention.

Having slept sporadically, Max was tired. His discussion with Amy had lingered in his mind. As he reclined his head against the seat cushion and closed his eyes, her face filled his memory, making him even more restive. Dozing was useless. He popped the latch of his briefcase and pulled out a file folder detailing the Dallas project, adamantly denying to himself that his attachment to Amy Holt was anything other than a creative solution to a sticky dilemma.

* * *

Once alone, Amy stared openmouthed at the check Max had left for the extra nights' lodging and meals. Even without the deposit, the amount was excessive, kindling her anxiety that she was nothing more than another business transaction for Max. He apparently thought he could buy anything—including her.

She glanced at the figures again. A week in a suite at the Warwick wouldn't cost this much, but then maybe he felt he owed her an amusement tax. His amusement, not hers. Amy was consumed with righteous indignation. How dare he trifle with her affections, then run off to some so-called emergency while leaving her a "tip."

She wished she'd had the courage to read him the riot act about how he'd wasted her time with nonsensical proposals and pretty words, playing mind games with other people's minds—specifically hers. Someone needed to inform Max Evans that sports of this kind were dangerous and victimizing.

Max had mentioned the elopement again before he left. So his proposal wasn't just a game, or if it was, one that he was playing out to the bitter end. But his motivations confused her more than ever. Less than a week ago, he was to marry Robin. No minor detail, that, to be swept like dirt under a rug. If he was even halfway sincere in his proposal to Amy, then there must be a hidden agenda at work. She had no inkling what to think or feel. All she knew was that she was, to paraphrase the old song, "bothered and bewildered."

She should take comfort in the fact Max was out of her life—at least temporarily—and concentrate on rebuilding her business without distractions. But it no longer seemed as simple as that. Amy felt empty, abandoned.

Using manual labor as a diversion, she allotted the afternoon to turning out the Hearts and Flowers Suite Max had occupied. Amy regularly employed a cleaning crew, but had canceled it in order to save money. Still, this was a job she liked to do, restoring the suite to its pristine condition after a guest had departed.

She'd taken satisfaction in securing the perfect furnishings for the room and the satisfaction was renewed each time she stepped across the threshold. She loved polishing the nineteenth-century dresser and fluffing the comforter and downy pillows.

Today the cleaning depressed her. The suite seemed barren. As she removed the sheets from the mahogany four-poster, Amy couldn't dismiss Max's lingering essence. Her chores were supposed to be a balm to her troubled spirit, but they weren't helping.

Be careful what you wish for. After all those days wanting Max out of her hair, now she was miserable without him. *Forget Max Evans and keep working.* There were a dozen weddings still left on the schedule, including one this next weekend. Plenty to do.

The ringing of the portable telephone she'd left in the bathroom jarred her and, hoping it was Max, Amy ran for it, stubbing her toe on the four-poster in her haste.

As she gave a frosty "not interested" to the telephone solicitor and slipped off her sandal, she chastised herself for responding as she'd done. Her reaction had been nothing less than that of a frenzied teenager madly sprinting to a call because it might be "him"—Mr. Wonderful finally making his move.

Amy had never been like this before. Her toe sent a throbbing clue to just how mindlessly she'd been behaving. Her sappy schoolgirl era had run its course and must come to an end. She wasn't going to spend one more second agonizing about Max Evans. The man had caused her nothing but grief. Now it was over. Finished.

Limping to her office, Amy decided to answer some correspondence, something she could accomplish with an elevated foot. The toe was swelling and she had to pamper it. She couldn't afford to be hobbling around. Not now.

The therapy was paying off and the throbbing abating somewhat when the phone rang again. Fortunately the telephone was right at her elbow—no danger of her acting the idiot and hurting herself to boot.

It was a business call and the message was more of the same—a cancellation. At least this bride was apologetic. "I'm sorry, but our friends are ribbing us so much about getting married at Torrence Place that I'm afraid it would ruin everything. My fiancé's mother doesn't have a sense of humor. I know we should laugh about it, but—"

"I understand." Amy tried to reassure the young woman. "Your wedding should be perfect. That's what you want and what I want for you. I can arrange another site if you'd like." Amy had been told, "We'll let you know." In her heart she knew she'd never hear from the couple again.

Now there were only eleven weddings left. Barely enough to support both her and Torrence Place. Ironically, those same eleven would also interfere with her seeking another job. Few employers would deign to work around her erratic calendar. Increased business for "Arrangements by Amy" was the only tack for her, and would take a while to bear fruit. If push came to shove, she'd just have to try for another loan—and beg the bank officer for mercy this go-round.

Of course, instead of a loan, she could cash Max's check. Sufficient money there to cover short-term losses.

But money she would never touch. To do so would be the same as being bought. And if she were willing to be bought, she might as well go whole hog and accept Max's proposal.

Despite her decision to cast it and him out of her thoughts, the absurd proposal kept popping into her head, her pulse running amok whenever she considered the possibility. *I'm glad he's gone. Truly I am.* If she said it often enough, maybe one day Amy would convince herself. Then this reckless infatuation would stop.

Unfortunately, the Max Evans assault on her senses continued when Amy switched on the television that evening. At the tail end of the six o'clock news was a shot of him at Hobby Airport. "Entrepreneur Max Evans was spotted this afternoon with accountant Melissa Meirs ready to board his private jet. When asked who or what was responsible for his recently canceled nuptials, Mr. Evans merely smiled. Some wonder if the attractive Ms. Meirs could be a contributing factor."

"Another woman?" Amy barked at the television set as she snapped it off. She felt more dismayed than ever.

A large vase of flowers arrived the next day. The blossoms were lovely, a mixture of colorful spring blooms, just the sort she favored. But the flowers didn't improve Amy's uncharitable disposition, nor did the enclosed card reading: "Thinking of you. Max." *I'll just bet. For five minutes maybe.*

"Pretty," Steph said, eyeing the flowers as she entered the kitchen Friday morning. Her nursing duties had taken precedence lately and Amy was so happy for the company she grabbed the other woman in an effusive hug. Dealing with Max's perfidy all week had been difficult. Without Stephanie, she'd been utterly miserable.

"Hey..." Stephanie backed up, holding Amy at arm's length for inspection. "Black clouds still on the horizon? I didn't mean to desert you, but I had a critical patient on my hands and was pulling twelve-hour shifts." She took a can of Diet Pepsi from the refrigerator and popped the tab. "Is your guest still around?"

"He left Monday."

"Too bad. I was hoping you were having fun in my absence. Flowers from anyone I know?"

"Max. A thank-you for the hospitality."

"You must have been *very* hospitable. That's an exquisite bouquet." She eyeballed Amy suspiciously.

"Uh, did you remember to put gas in the van?" Amy hedged.

"Yes, I did, oh evasive one," Stephanie replied good-humoredly.

Amy was glad Steph had taken no offense. While she was the dearest of friends, Amy knew better than to share too much while she harbored such confusion over Max. Steph was the type to wax ecstatic about a possible match, to jump to all the wrong conclusions.

"Whatever his motives, they're very cheery," Stephanie continued, undeterred.

"It would take more than flowers to cheer me up. I'm too far down in the doldrums," Amy said. "After tonight's ceremony, there are only ten weddings left."

"Another couple reneged?"

Amy nodded. "But only one, so maybe everything's quieting down."

"I'm sure it is. Now tell me one more thing about Max. How did you manage to evict him?"

"Didn't have to. He left on his own. Said Evans Enterprises needed him." Amy could sense that Stephanie wanted details, that she wasn't satisfied with this abridged version, but for once Steph didn't press her and the hours passed pleasantly as the two bustled about getting ready for the approaching festivities.

The Friday evening rites were complete and the reception in full swing when Stephanie whispered to Amy, "Look who's here," and motioned across the room to Max standing under a bower of greenery. He held a beer in his hand, an arm casually arced around Jenna Peters's shoulder.

Amy felt a stab of jealousy, which was quickly matched by fury. So much for his promise to call. *The rat*. Evidently, Amy Holt hadn't been top priority on his list of contacts when he returned from his business trip. How long had he been back, anyway? She had no way of knowing.

Not only was Max beguiling Jenna, but several other women had formed a circle and were hanging on his every word. "The man seems to bounce between women faster than a tennis ball at Wimbledon," she muttered to Stephanie.

"Those vultures. Someone ought to race over there and yank him out of their clutches. Someone like you."

"You're certainly aggressive with *my* behavior." Amy was amazed her voice was so calm when she was seething inside.

"Okay, then just go say hello."

"It's bad form to mingle with the guests," Amy replied, her eyes still on Max. *Furthermore, I intend to avoid this particular guest like an open flame*. She'd already been seared once.

During the last year she'd done several high-profile Houston weddings, but Amy didn't recall Max at any of them. It was just like him to show up now—the proverbial bad penny. She could only hope he'd be too busy flirting with Jenna and others who wanted to comfort him in his hour of need to notice her.

Just at that instant, his head turned in her direction and Amy knew he saw her. Feeling a rush of adrenaline, a fight-or-flight panic, she darted into the kitchen. The buffet table needed replenishing.

She was placing parsley around an aspic mold when Max slipped up behind her. Somehow she knew he was there even before he spoke. "Hello," he said. "I didn't realize you'd be here tonight. No wonder you weren't home when I called."

"You called?" Amy replied coolly, glancing up at him.

"About five. You must have been on your way here. I left a message."

"Then promptly dialed the next person on your list? Does Jenna know she wasn't number one?"

Nonchalantly Max leaned against the refrigerator, hands in the pockets of his suit pants. "Looks as though business is recovering," he responded, sidestepping her impertinent question. "Is hard work the reason for your testiness?"

"Business is booming," Amy answered. "Almost too good to be true." In fact, not true at all, but she felt the need to maintain as upbeat an illusion as possible. It hardly seemed fair that he could be so fit and happy, in stark contrast to her state of total distress.

"If things are so good, then why do I detect a mountain of tension in you—like nitro about to blow? If it's not business, then missing me must be the cause of your anxiety." He came up to her and started massaging the knotted muscles at the base of her neck.

"I wouldn't waste an ounce of energy missing a man so fickle he probably needs a scorecard to remember who's in his arms."

Max turned her around and eased her into an embrace. "Want to test me? Right now, I'm holding the only woman I have any desire to hold." His words and the magic of his eyes made her forget both her rancor and the dwindling buffet table. She snuggled closer. For days she'd needed a shoulder to lean on and here it was, broad and inviting.

Then she remembered herself and jerked away from the temptation before her. If it weren't for Max and the chaos he'd created, she wouldn't need any shoulders but her own.

"It's just the strain from all the new demands," she said. Demands like the housecleaning and doing double duty to replace the maid she ordinarily hired for functions such as tonight's reception. To say nothing of wrestling with the confusion caused by the man who was now a breath away.

"I'm a master at strains." He took her face in his palms and brushed his lips across hers.

Amy backed away. "Don't play with me, Max. I'm not an idiot. You were carrying on with half a dozen admirers just minutes ago."

Max grinned. "Was I?"

Amy didn't respond. In truth, the admirers were doing more of the carrying-on, but that was irrelevant.

"I assure you there was no carrying-on on my part," he said.

"Not even with your date?"

"I don't have a date, merely a family obligation. You have those occasionally, too, I'd bet." He reached for her again.

"Forget the seduction bit," Amy said. "I'm no longer susceptible to your tactics of temptation."

"Did it ever occur to you that you're the temptress...and that I'm *extremely* susceptible?" He cradled the nape of her neck and gently drew her closer, his hands tantalizingly tracing her spine as they slowly slid to her waist. "Let—"

"Oh, excuse me!" Stephanie burst into the kitchen, followed a couple of paces behind by Jenna and the hostess, Phyllis Wilcox. "I came for more deviled shrimp." Stephanie held up an empty bowl.

Amy was so embarrassed she could feel a hot rush all the way to her toes. It wouldn't take much imagination for Mrs. Wilcox to deduce that her caterer was neglecting her tasks to frolic in the kitchen with a male guest. Worse, the society matron would likely spread the word to all her friends, aided and abetted by Jenna. Another nail in the coffin of "Arrangements by Amy." *Why did Max have to come on to me while I was working?* Once again, Amy's problems could be laid directly at Max's feet.

"I was telling the caterer how much I enjoy your parties," Max told Mrs. Wilcox, giving his hostess a beguiling smile. "The food is always sublime."

"Mrs. Wilcox's selections for the reception were wonderful, weren't they?" Amy said, grasping for any lifeline, even one thrown out by Max.

Max's ploy succeeded and Phyllis Wilcox beamed. Amy knew she'd barely avoided a devastating mishap, but that didn't make her feel one speck of appreciation for Max's diverting her client's attention. She was still too furious over being put in a compromising position in the first place. "Now I'm sure you all want to get back to the happy couple," she said, daring to exhale when the trio of Max, Mrs. Wilcox and Jenna took the hint and left the kitchen, followed by Stephanie.

Amy's next two hours were spent suppressing thoughts of Max, while trying to see to her duties. She was loading the last of her supplies in the company van, about to make her exit when he approached her in the driveway. "Have dinner with me tomorrow."

"I'm busy tomorrow."

"Sunday, then."

"Busy then, too. Go away before Mrs. Wilcox spots you."

"Phyllis is at the front door bidding her guests goodnight."

"I don't care." She wasn't going to be ensnared again. It might take a while to liberate her senses from Max, but Amy was dead set on nipping temptation in the bud and never allowing it to reflower. "Leave me alone and go back to your date."

He laughed.

Amy was not amused. "Or has Jenna already been promoted to fiancée? You are awfully anxious to trot down the aisle." Amy knew she sounded petty, but she couldn't stop herself.

"What a poor opinion you have of me. Determined to think I'm so desperate for a wife that anyone in a skirt will do. Tsk, tsk. And after I've assured you that you're the bride for me."

"How many times do I have to tell you that I'm not going to be your bride? I repeat, leave me alone."

"If it weren't so trite, I'd say how cute you look when you're angry." He brushed his knuckles down her cheek.

Amy swatted his hand away. She wasn't going to be seduced by his facile flattery or his coaxing caresses. Not anymore. She thrust her chin out. "Good night, Max." Pulling her keys from the pocket of her skirt, Amy got into the van. Luck was with her tonight. Steph had already left in her own car and Amy was able to make a clean getaway, leaving Max standing in the drive as she sped off.

When Amy arrived home, her answering machine was blinking with the earlier message from Max. "I recognize your contempt for my money, however, I made loads of it on this Dallas contract and need some help spending it. What do you say to Paris this weekend? Paris, France, or Paris, Texas, your choice. Call me later tonight." He rattled off his home number. "By the way, I had wonderful dreams in Dallas...help me make them come true."

Over the next two days, Amy replayed the message often enough to nearly wear out the tape. It took all her resolve not to phone Max's number. Each time she began to weaken, she reminded herself that yes, he had called, but had then proceeded to find someone else when she was busy. Hardly a picture of an enamored lover.

No one booked a wedding the next week, but no one dropped one, either. More important, the meeting planner for one of Houston's large oil corporations inquired about holding a series of small staff retreats at Torrence Place and invited Amy to submit a bid. Finally, a ray of sunshine.

Business meetings were a superb source of income. Convention activities, too. If she hadn't been in such an emotional turmoil over Max, Amy would have already been beating the bushes for such events. A preference for weddings didn't preclude exploring other money-making avenues. Drastic times called for drastic measures. Resuscitating her wedding business might take a while but that didn't mean "Arrangements by Amy" had to go under in the interim.

She spotted Stephanie cutting flowers and ivy in the garden and went out to share the good news. As Stephanie made her floral selections and Amy held the flower basket, they chatted about developing the bid as well as a new brochure to send to other Houston companies. Once the basket was filled, they went inside, Stephanie carrying the overflowing cuttings and Amy gingerly holding the stems of an assortment of roses.

"I'll arrange these. You get to your office."

"As soon as I check the mail. Who knows what it'll bring—perhaps a notice that I've won the sweepstakes." Amy opened the front door and had fished her mail out of the box when Max's car arrived at the curb. She wanted to scurry back inside and instruct Stephanie to tell him she wasn't home. It was too late for that, however, since Max had already seen her.

"Hi," he said, walking up. "Am I disturbing you?"

You always disturb me was her silent response. "Why are you here?" she managed instead.

"To see you, of course. Since you were so 'busy' this weekend that you couldn't even return my phone call, I didn't chance being ignored again."

Dummy. You should have bolted after all. Yet Amy knew she could as easily have flown to the moon. All weekend, she'd longed for him, wondering if she'd let a siege of jealousy and false pride lead her down the wrong path. Then she remembered his dismal track record with women.

When Stephanie appeared out of nowhere and tapped her on the shoulder, Amy, now totally unhinged by her conflicting emotions, almost leapt into Max's arms.

"Didn't mean to sneak up on you. Just wanted to let you know the flowers are fixed," Steph said. "Hi, Max. Sorry to run off, but I have, uh...laundry to do. Bye, Max." She left.

Stephanie is as subtle as a runaway train, Amy thought. *Uh...laundry, indeed*. She looked at Max. "You didn't tell me what you wanted."

Her tone was no-nonsense, but Max paid no attention, taking full advantage of the opening line. "You," he growled suggestively. "I want you."

"All the other women in your life busy?"

"I've given up other women."

"Since Friday night?" Amy deliberately added soft laughter to show Max it meant nothing to her. "Considering all that attention I received from you this weekend, it's obvious how much you want me." *Darn.* She hadn't meant to say that.

"Which way do you want it, Amy?" He was leaning over her, his arm propped above her head. "Your parting shot in the Wilcox driveway was that I should leave you alone and you've given me no indication since that you've changed your mind. It took all the manly nerve I could muster to stop by and risk rejection again."

His soulful expression almost brought a giggle to Amy's lips, but he wasn't going to get around her so easily. "Do you particularly enjoy harassing me or can't you find anything better to do today?" she asked as a countermeasure.

"I didn't realize this was harassment. Actually, I was wondering about lunch. Since I seem to be drawn to this neighborhood for some strange reason, I decided to check out a shopping center, then see if I could talk you into a meal."

Having a shopping trip take precedence over her wasn't particularly complimentary, nevertheless, she was hungry, too. She'd breakfasted early and forgotten all about lunch. *No*, she admonished. Amy knew it was in her best interests to rebuff him and spend the afternoon working on that bid. "You're out of luck on lunch. The cupboard's bare and the cook's busy. Afraid you'll just have to run to a McDonald's."

He laughed. "I wasn't asking you to feed me, just keep me company. The noon crowd at the Spanish Flower should have thinned out by now. Come be my guest for a change. It's one of my favorite places. What do you say?"

I say go away. That's what her head told her to answer, but Amy listened to her heart, which sent an entirely different message.

Less than fifteen minutes later, she was sitting across from Max, sipping a margarita and laughing about his recounting of a business meeting that morning. One of the scions of the Houston corporate world had fallen asleep and snored through the entire session. "We were all wondering whether his snores should be recorded in the official transcript."

As the meal progressed, Amy couldn't resist boasting of her call from the meeting planner. Max was appropriately enthusiastic, giving her a thumbs-up. "That's great," he said. "Only I'm chagrined I didn't suggest something like that myself. I'd like a retreat at Torrence Place, too. That is, if you think you could put up with me."

"I wasn't bucking for your business."

"Now you wouldn't turn me down, would you, Amy?" He took her hand.

"Experience has taught me to be very leery of business deals with you," she answered, trying to keep the conversation impersonal even though both of them understood that Max had changed the subject and was no longer referring to Evans Enterprises or "Arrangements by Amy."

"Is marrying me a business deal?"

"We weren't talking marriage."

"Weren't we?" Max's smile was potent, potent enough to reverse the Gulf tides.

"To be honest, that topic frightens me," she admitted.

"Amy Holt, the expert on weddings, terrified over her own? Incredible."

"Still, that's how I feel. How can you not be afraid? We met under bizarre circumstances and we don't know each other that well."

"Well enough. Or is there some sort of timetable I'm not aware of? Do a prescribed number of days need to pass between introduction and wedding day? Am I supposed to court you for a year, then steal a kiss goodnight, and after another year has elapsed, drum up the courage to ask your father for your hand? I thought you were the romantic, Amy. Can you honestly tell me you don't believe in love at first sight?"

Amy shook her head in dismay. "This from the man who claims not to believe in love at all. If I had an ounce of good sense, I'd run out of this restaurant like my hair was on fire."

"But you're not going to, are you?" He'd just brushed her hand with his lips when Robin Porter walked into the restaurant.

CHAPTER EIGHT

"WHAT exactly is going on?" Amy demanded. "Why is *she* here?"

Max twisted his head around to follow Amy's gaze. When he saw Robin, he turned back. "Amy, I—"

Before he could say anything further, Robin strolled up to their table. She was accompanied by a young sandy-haired man who kept slightly away from the group. "My, my, how...fascinating," Robin purred. "The wedding planner is still on the job even though there's no wedding."

"This isn't what you think," Amy protested weakly, as Robin shot her a telling glance. The role of the "other woman" was not one she'd aspired to play and she was chagrined at being portrayed as such.

Robin focused her attention on Max. "No wonder you seemed to be losing interest, darling." She patted his cheek, her crimson fingernails bloodlike against his skin.

"Nice tan," Max said flippantly, turning a deaf ear to her taunt. "Your TV coverage must be waning. I didn't realize you were back from the beaches of Mexico." Unlike Amy, he didn't act at all disturbed by Robin's innuendos. Rather he sounded amazingly unruffled.

Amy decided to take her cue from him. The woman had lost all claims on Max and if she was looking for scapegoats, a mirror was a good place to start. On the day of the wedding, she'd appeared as willing as her fiancé to forgo their scheduled ceremony. Maybe more willing, considering she'd been a near no-show. Max Evans was now a free man with all strings severed.

For moments no one spoke, the four frozen awkwardly in place. Eventually Robin's escort came closer, extended a hand and introduced himself. Not the same escort with Robin in Mexico. *Hmm, three men in a matter of weeks*. Like Max, the woman had been busy lining up replacements. Yes, Amy thought, she definitely had no gripe coming.

Robin, however, didn't seem to grasp that fact. Amy was astonished when she pulled out a chair and sat down. "Why don't we make it a foursome?" she said, motioning for her escort to sit, also.

He did as bidden, but there was a trace of pink at his collar giving evidence of discomfort. After a bit of meaningless chatter and some questioning glances from Robin to Amy, Max signaled for a check. Happily, the action prompted Robin and friend to seek another table. "Okay, we'll move along if you're going to run out," she chided, and the pair selected a site by a window.

"Sorry about that. She can say and do the damnedest things." Max fished out a credit card from his wallet and flipped it onto the table, the attentive waiter scooping it up and returning promptly with the receipt.

Once they were out of the restaurant, Amy spoke. "Was that 'accidental' meeting really an accident?" She knew coincidences occurred, but needed reassurance that Max had been as taken aback by Robin's showing up as she.

His forehead knitted in a frown. "How could you think anything else? As you saw with what's-his-name—that kid she had in tow—Robin hasn't let a blade of grass grow under her feet, romance-wise. And as for me, I have no desire to see or talk to her."

"Or to make her jealous?"

"That's not even in the equation. I thought you knew me enough by now to understand that Robin plays no part in my life anymore."

"What part do I have?" Amy asked, still disconcerted by the afternoon's happenings. Max had answered her concerns, but a sliver of suspicion lingered. She needed more convincing. "When you talk about a closer relationship—"

"Yes," he interrupted, "I'd definitely call marriage a closer relationship." He opened the car door and helped Amy inside, leaning over her to add, "I thought I'd made it plain what part I want you to have."

Max circled the Lexus and seated himself at the driver's wheel, then turned her way, propping an elbow on the back of his seat, the car keys dangling from one finger. "I know you're unsure about all this."

"More than unsure," Amy admitted. "Frankly, it doesn't seem real. I get the impression you're playacting and I'm an understudy unexpectedly cast in the lead...who knows for how long."

"I'm not acting and there's no way I'd let you be replaced. I've told you some of the reasons I want a wife—to share my life, to bear my children, to fill a void...

"That's not all of it though. Frankly, I'm not certain I know all the reasons myself. Something deep within tells me that the two of us finding one another is a stroke of luck we need to take advantage of or we'll both regret it. You're the one for me. Give us a chance, Amy."

That little flutter rose in her heart again. "Why am I the one?" she whispered. She wanted the *words*. The "I love you." He smiled as if amused. "Well, because I'm a guy and you're a gal—that's usually a good basis for getting together." Transferring the keys to the ignition, he began playing with a strand of her reddish blond hair, wrapping it around his finger.

"That premise established, what do you have in mind?"

Max beat a tattoo against the steering wheel as he thought. "Maybe we need to begin all over. Be conventional, go out on a date, a movie, the theater, whatever. Afterward, a nightcap. Then I walk you to your door and kiss you good-night...like this." He leaned closer and brushed his lips against hers.

At first, Amy gave in to the kiss, savoring Max's touch, then feeling a need for air, she turned her head. It was then she saw Robin scowling at them from inside the restaurant. "Is all this for the benefit of the audience?" Amy gestured toward the window.

Max followed her line of vision and without a word started the car and shifted into drive. They rode three or four blocks before he pulled over to the curb and cut the engine. "Satisfied? There's no audience." He ran a fingertip along the plane of her cheek. "Now where were we? Ah, yes, dating, the good-night kiss..."

Amy pressed herself against the door handle, withdrawing from him. Max's eyes said too much. Dating definitely wasn't foremost on his mind. "Is all that before or after we run off to Nevada?" she asked tartly, determined to disregard Max's kisses and the way they made her feel all warm and willing.

"Either way you want it," he said. "We can get married first and kiss later. Or we can practice everything now, perfect our technique in advance."

"Everything? Just what will you include in those practice sessions?" She could think of several things...all appealing, too darn appealing. If only he were the teeniest bit in love with her. *Love*. For all Max's attempts to sway her, he'd conscientiously avoided that particular four-letter word. She needed to remember that and keep her wits about her. Amy eyed him suspiciously.

"Why do I have the impression you'd take full advantage of the 'everything'?"

"Have I taken advantage of you, Amy?"

"You mean other than staying where you were unwanted?"

"'Unwanted.' Are you certain about that?" He sounded cold and arrogant, much like the Max of old. But the wounded expression that flashed across his face belied the frosty pose.

Amy touched his sleeve. "That was rude of me. I didn't mean to hurt your feelings."

A sardonic smile greeted her statement. "I'd gotten the impression you don't credit me with having feelings."

Max's impression was near correct—until a second ago anyway. Still Amy felt compelled to deny it. "You misread me."

"Like you've been misreading me?" he asked, switching on the motor. "Don't you think we should clear up your confusion once and for all? What exactly are you so concerned about, Amy?" His tone was now accusatory.

Lots of things. "For starters, why you allegedly were hiding out at Torrence Place to avoid the press. You weren't camera-shy at Hobby Airport."

"So you saw the TV clip." He cut the engine again.

"Yes, and you looked quite comfortable, smug even."

"All an act. I couldn't very well come across like a whipped dog, now could I?" He leaned against the door, watching her intently. "I was hoping you didn't see it—afraid you might conclude Melissa and I were off on a rendezvous instead of tending to business."

Although the thought had crossed her mind, Amy wasn't about to tell Max so. "Isn't she your accountant?" *An attractive, sexy accountant.*

"Yeah, and a darn good one, too. That's the reason I took her along. I needed her advice, her expertise. As I told you, we saved the project. A hotel complex in the area of DFW Airport."

"I'm glad everything worked out. But that still doesn't answer my question about your motives for staying at Torrence Place. Or really explain your abrupt departure."

"I suppose my motives were mixed. I preferred to hide out until the flak died down, thinking Robin would be equally inaccessible. And I can't deny it gave me a chance to get to know you better." His hand circled her neck, his thumb gently grazing an earlobe. "As I told you, I left because of a critical business situation. But, Amy—"

"Yes?"

"You must know that even without the emergency, it was time for me to go."

"I know," she said, trying unsuccessfully to ignore his grip. "After all, I'd asked you to leave often enough."

"But that was for self-protection, wasn't it?"

"I don't understand what you mean," she said.

"I think you do. You know exactly what would have happened if I'd stayed longer."

"I do?"

"Don't be coy, Amy. Things between us were becoming too hot to handle, so I slacked off, giving you space to grow more amenable to my proposal. I hoped that you'd had enough space by now. Tell me, have you come to your senses and decided to marry me after all?" Those blue-violet eyes were gleaming like two perfect gems.

Amy exhaled loudly. "We aren't ready for that kind of commitment. Just a few minutes ago, we were exploring a first date and..." She was leading right back to those kisses.

"You never run out of excuses, do you? 'Don't know each other well enough... aren't ready...' Maybe you aren't ready, but I am. So what can I do to hurry up the process and claim to know Amy Holt? Let's see how good I am at guessing. Your favorite color is blue."

"Pink."

"You're allergic to strawberries."

"Penicillin."

"You listen to hard rock."

"The old big band music," she returned, recognizing that he was making sport. "Thus far you're batting zero."

"So I've got a lot to learn about you. Think how much fun you'll have enlightening me. It'll be an adventure discovering all those things. By the way, I'm also allergic to penicillin. We have more in common than you realized."

Amy sighed. "We have nothing in common where it counts. You have more money than Midas and I'm a small business owner, a struggling one at that. You play in society and I work in society. Just the opposite from me. You don't believe in love and I want a man who loves me so much that he can't bear waking up in the morning without me at his side. You have this *comme ci, comme ça* attitude toward marriage while I want a marriage bond so strong that neither partner would ever consider a future complete without the other in the picture."

"You want guarantees." Max's tone had gone chilly again. He turned the ignition key, signaling an end to the conversation.

Amy wasn't to be deterred. "Yes, I suppose I do."

"Hasn't anyone ever told you that life holds no guarantees?"

"Yes, but I've always refused to believe it, especially when it comes to love, true love."

They pulled into the driveway at Torrence Place and Max opened his door. Amy did the same, and he walked her up the front steps, his palm resting casually against the small of her back, as though the disagreement had never happened. When they arrived at the threshold, she stopped and thanked him politely for lunch. Under the circumstances, Amy hadn't expected his smile. Or his scorching kiss—right there on the porch, in front of God, man and all her neighbors.

"So long, sugar. I'll call you."

"Please don't," she said, escaping into the house before he could protest.

So she'd told him not to call—when had Max really heeded her ultimatums? Almost a week had passed since their lunch together and he'd telephoned daily, always from a different city. He was on a marathon inspection of properties in a half-dozen places.

Feeling the hypocrite, Amy welcomed the calls. Max seemed to have accepted her complaint that they weren't ready for a long-term commitment and had determined they needed to get better acquainted fast.

In addition to the calls, he sent flowers—not once, but twice. A man in hot pursuit of a goal.

"I wish he'd stop this nonsense," she told Stephanie, snipping the stem of an exotic blossom and standing it in a tall urn.

"It is pretty inconsiderate," Stephanie agreed dryly, "sending flowers...calling long-distance every night—"

"But what does it all really mean?" Amy interrupted, her insecurities surfacing. "So Max has sent a few flowers...that's nothing for a man of his means and likely a chore he relegated to his secretary."

"*She* didn't make the phone calls."

"Traveling can be lonely. He just wants someone to talk to."

"Like that'd be a problem for a babe magnet like Max."

"Don't remind me. That's the part that's so bothersome."

"Glory be!" Stephanie shouted. "How thick-skulled can I be? You've fallen for the guy!"

"I didn't say that."

"You didn't have to. Only it's just now sinking in. All that impatience with Robin, your reaction to Jenna Peters, even the way you've been fondling that bird of paradise bloom says it loud and clear. I was beginning to wonder about you, lady. The super-desirable Max Evans pursuing you and your trying to ward him off. It backfired, didn't it? You're in love!"

Amy speared another bird of paradise into the vase. "What difference does it make if I am? He's out of my reach. Besides, I have serious doubts whether he can settle down. He says he wants to, but who knows? Everywhere he goes he seems to be in the company of rich beautiful women. How can I be sure of a man like that...? Oh, can't we talk about something more pleasant?"

Steph agreeably changed the subject to the big news they'd been handed right before the delivery of the flowers. "A week of meetings, you said. That's great."

"I could hardly believe my ears," Amy answered, attempting to sound jubilant. "I only dropped off the contract day before yesterday. Didn't expect a response until the end of the month. Then when the meeting planner rang me up saying ours was the winning offer...well!'' She paused a moment to take a deep breath and to calculate in her head. ''Of course, I bid at rock bottom.''

''Where does that put 'Arrangements by Amy'?''

''At a minimum it makes up for a couple of wedding commissions. In fact, it frees up money for a shopping expedition, if you're in the mood. I could use some new clothes. There has to be a sale somewhere.'' Amy went in search of the newspaper.

Her attention was captured not by an ad for dresses half-off, but by an article about an art gallery opening. It featured an accompanying photograph of Max with Robin Porter. ''Has the dueling duo made up?'' read the caption. Amy passed the newspaper to Stephanie. ''See what I mean.''

''Pooh,'' Stephanie said, shoving the section aside and grabbing another one with a department store ad. ''You can't believe everything you read in the papers. If all the news was gospel, then Torrence Place should be labeled a wedding safety hazard. Remember?''

''I guess you're right.'' Amy once more forced cheer into her tone. ''So, what are we waiting for? The cash registers beckon.''

Trying to prove to herself and her friend she was taking this latest episode with Max in her stride, Amy bought two dresses, a pair of shorts and a T-shirt. Then, since Jay had hospital duty, she insisted on treating Stephanie to a movie and dinner. It was after nine when they got home and parted at the rear gate.

Amy's phone was ringing when she entered through the kitchen door. She'd have preferred to let the answering machine handle the call, but suspected it was

Max and knew she would only be delaying the inevitable. "Hello," she said cautiously.

"Hi, there. I'm lying on the couch thinking how nice it would be if you were here with me." There was a lazy, sensual quality to his voice. "I've been calling since seven. You haven't been stepping out on me, have you?"

"What if I have? We aren't going steady."

"We can whenever you're ready."

"I can't get too excited about the prospect when every time I pick up the newspaper I spot you with another female. In today's *Chronicle* it's a recycled one—your former fiancée. If you're not careful, Max, you're going to be tripping over brides."

"Ah, now I see what's causing the edge in your voice. First, let's put something to rest. Robin Porter will never—never, I repeat—be my bride. Second, if you'll cool down for a second, you'll remember that I invited you to that gallery opening. You had a previous engagement. Or at least that's what you told me."

"I had a wedding consultation. Considering the damage my business has recently suffered, I didn't have the luxury of canceling it. You wasted no time finding a stand-in for me."

"But I didn't. I can't control who comes to these affairs. I—"

Amy hung up. In five more seconds, Max'd be spinning some cock-and-bull story about him and Robin, and fool that she was, she'd probably buy into the tale. Whatever he said, two coincidental meetings with Robin Porter was one coincidence too many. Besides, she'd seen that newspaper photo—Robin was hanging on Max like Spanish moss and definitely not looking the part of an ex-fiancée.

The phone rang again. Amy left it to the recorder, replaying the message as soon as the call ended. It was

Max finishing his aborted sentence, "—didn't have a date with—or encourage—Robin. Goodbye."

"Goodbye" sounded rather final. Amy hit the erase button. She didn't care to hear the message a second time. Tears welled in her eyes and she blinked them away. She wasn't going to cry over Max. He wasn't worth her tears, or a pair of red eyes. Tomorrow was a workday, an important day on the dwindling calendar of weddings.

Her van loaded with paraphernalia, Amy made her way to the site of the ceremony, the River Oaks estate of Emily Southmore and her parents. It wasn't far from the Evans family address. "Forget Max," Amy muttered aloud as she wound down Kirby Lane and turned on Chevy Chase. But the thought crossed her mind that he could be at the service. Her nerves were already frazzled with the specter of something going awry; it hardly seemed fair that she might have to contend with Max, too. *Concentrate on your job*, Amy lectured herself. *You have no jurisdiction over anything else. Especially Max*.

Focusing on her work didn't relax Amy one whit. Even though she'd completed two weddings since Max and Robin's, her confidence level hadn't risen. She'd never been preoccupied with a ceremony falling apart, having been of a mind that, despite the inevitable small glitches, the final product was always an idyllic fantasy, made to order for each happy couple. Now Amy's faith in happy couples and their fantasies had been overridden by a sense of impending doom.

When she drove through the massive wrought-iron gates at the Southmore Estate, the crew she'd hired was already there, erecting tents on the grounds for the reception, a catered dinner for three hundred guests.

As the musicians launched into the wedding processional later that afternoon, Amy crossed her fingers.

Today the precaution was unnecessary. Emily drifted down the aisle as ethereally as a fairy-tale princess, and Barry Osborne, her groom, grinned adoringly as his bride completed the walk to his side.

When their voices broke during recitation of the vows, Amy choked up, too. This was what it was all about. This was why she'd suffer marital meltdowns like the one between Robin and Max to keep "Arrangements by Amy" afloat.

She emitted a prayer of thanks that business prospects were encouraging. Just before leaving the house that morning, she'd been contacted by the owners of a local computer firm. Having learned about the corporate sessions, they'd asked to meet with her to plan some of their own. Another five days of retreats were in the bag. Word of mouth was bringing in new customers and brochures, once disseminated, would generate even more.

Amy would soon be on firm financial footing again and able to begin the next phase of Torrence Place renovations. She felt more optimistic that the wedding business would slowly return, also. Watching the cake cutting from the side of the main tent, Amy heaved a giant sigh of relief.

The relief faded abruptly as she saw Robin Porter approaching the newlyweds. This Houston social whirl was getting too small for comfort. Amy'd given little thought to Robin today, probably because she was overwrought by the possibility of Max being a guest. It hadn't occurred to her that she might have to deal with both of them at once. Not again.

But so far she hadn't seen Max. Perhaps she'd luck out and he wouldn't show. At that precise moment, Amy spied him with Jenna. As the two headed for the receiving line, they were laughing and talking, unknowingly embarked on a collision course with Robin.

Amy waited wide-eyed for the inevitable explosion, but none occurred. There were amicable greetings and smiles all around, then the trio moved on a few paces to speak with Emily and Barry. Amy couldn't figure out the dynamics. Robin had acted like a petulant child with her and Max at the restaurant. Why then so peaceable today? Likely on her best behavior because she was surrounded by many mutual acquaintances and of a mind that this was no place to throw a snit.

A tantrum of her own began to seem downright appealing as the reception continued and Amy's frustration mounted. Max was waltzing with Jenna on the dance floor. Although Amy tried to console herself with the knowledge that it wasn't Robin in his arms, she couldn't suppress her displeasure. Here he was flanked by his almost wife, new girlfriend and former wedding consultant. Worse still, he'd asked woman number three—Amy—to elope with him. Even without that last tidbit, the four of them made a perfect combination to reactivate the destructive gossip, Amy thought, glancing nervously around the tented room.

Fear meshed with actuality when Max left Jenna at the edge of the dance floor and moved Amy's way. *Oh, no.* The last time she'd talked to Max, she'd hung up on him and he'd been none too happy about it. It would be her luck for him to use the situation for meting out some public punishment. Amy had no intention of giving him that chance. She executed a fast one-hundred-and-eighty-degree turn in the other direction, but Max was speedier, catching up with her before she could duck outside the tent.

"Stephanie told me you'd be here. I figured coming to Emily's wedding would force you to talk to me."

"Stephanie's mouth gets bigger by the day. I may have to resort to murder to silence her."

"No way. I thank my guardian angel for Stephanie and her big mouth," Max answered, grabbing Amy's hand. "Dance with me."

"You know I can't."

"Can't dance?" His eyes glimmered. "It's a slow number. All you need to do is lean on me, shuffle your feet and no one will notice."

"Quit being obtuse. I don't need dance lessons. If I get on that floor with you, believe me, people *will* notice. You're still gossip fodder."

"Who cares?"

"I do. 'Arrangements by Amy' is beginning to recover from all the notoriety and I'm not going to feed the association between me and marital catastrophe. One more slip and I'll be the Typhoid Mary of the wedding industry. I'll be lucky even to be *invited to a wedding*."

"Well, then, you'd better dance with me—otherwise I'm likely to do something guaranteed to ignite the crowd."

"Like what?"

"Like kissing you...the way I've been wanting to kiss you all week while we've been apart." His hand slid up her arm. "In fact, I think I'd rather do that than dance."

Amy lifted a hand to signal "stop." "Okay, you win. Let's dance. One brief, circumspect dance." *And hope that the Southmores won't mind.*

Max held her closely, but not intimately; still Amy could feel the eyes of an audience. She tried to purge her mind of them, but it was useless. She was too aware—of the onlookers, the frowning disapproval of her client, but most of all...of Max.

"What are you doing when this is over?" he asked as the music subsided.

"I doubt I'll be finished before midnight."

He raised a skeptical eyebrow.

"Cleaning up takes a long while," she said defensively. "We'll have to disassemble the tents, pack away—"

"I'll wait. I'll even roll up my sleeves and help."

"That's not necessary. Besides, you have to take Jenna home."

"I can come back."

"No thanks. I get the impression Jenna Peters is important to you. I suggest you give her more of your attention instead of trying to spread it around like horse manure." When the band started a new song, Amy scooted away, successfully exiting the tent.

Persistent as ever, Max followed her, wrapping an arm around her waist as she walked toward the catering trailer. "Jenna is important," he agreed good-naturedly. "But she'll understand. She won't mind if I return."

Amy shook off his arm and faced him, her fists clenched at her sides. "*I* mind. Maybe this is how life is with your set, but I'm not so blasé, so Hollywood. Leave me alone, Max."

"That's one thing I can't do," he said, ambling off.

CHAPTER NINE

WOULD this function never end? Until then, with every step she took, every move she made, she'd be anguishing about Max saying or doing something outrageous. Amy felt as jittery as a vet-bound Chihuahua.

Ladies' man or no, did Max honestly think he could juggle dates with two women in one night? And why? Acknowledging Jenna as important to him, he'd supported that statement by his actions. From Amy's perspective, Jenna received much more deference than Robin ever had, yet here Max was, ready to dump her for the evening in order to pursue a dalliance with Amy.

It wasn't in Amy's nature to be drawn into a triangle or quadrangle or whatever it was Max had in mind, because, denials aside, he might not have Robin out of his system.

The man was one hundred and one percent trouble. He'd almost single-handedly wrecked her business, then tormented her unmercifully and—she might as well admit it—bruised her heart in the bargain. Well, the business was recovering, the aggravation could be dealt with, and Amy would not allow that bruise to turn into a massive hemorrhage. Whatever Max asked of her from now on, the answer was going to be no. A loud resounding no.

Halfway across the lawn, she noticed Jenna coming her way, determination written on her face. *What now?* Obviously Jenna had seen them dancing—who could have missed it? Was she intent on confronting Amy about Max's attentions? Jenna might not be the type to create a scene, but it was a risk Amy couldn't take. Besides, she'd spent too many hours already putting up with Max Evans's women.

A crowd of people mingled nearby and Amy blended in with them, only a temporary evasion, however, for twice more during the festivities Jenna attempted to corner her. In each instance Amy made a counteracting detour and avoided her. By the time the reception was over and the guests had departed, she felt as if she'd spent the day hiking in the rugged Big Bend Country bordering Mexico.

Her headlights illuminating the front porch revealed Max sprawled lazily in the wooden swing. Amy parked in the drive and glanced over his way. A cardboard box filled with Chinese food containers sat beside him.

Amy wished she could curb the stupid streak of emotion which kept sabotaging her. All reason said she should be angry, ready to lash out at Max—not pleased to find him waiting for her. But the streak wouldn't be denied.

Max looked rugged and handsome, wedding attire exchanged for boots, thigh-hugging Levi's and a Western-styled shirt, sleeves rolled to the elbow. Slightly weak-kneed, she climbed from the vehicle and walked over to the porch.

"Tired?"

"Exhausted." Amy suddenly became aware of how droopy she must appear. Her hair had surrendered to the Houston humidity, and her flax-colored linen suit was wrinkled and stained with cranberry punch spilled on her by an apologetic guest. Even though she'd worn low-heeled pumps, her feet were killing her.

Max grabbed his box of food and stood up. "Why don't you change into something more comfortable while I make us a drink."

"Rum and Coke," she said, unlocking the door and leading him inside. Amy decided on a fast shower to wash away the grime and the tension of the day. Feeling slightly better after the shower's stinging spray, she dried off, then freshened her makeup. Dressed in walking shorts and a cotton blouse, she sought out Max in the kitchen.

He handed her the rum and Coke and joined her at the table, opening cartons containing an assortment of oriental entrées. "I didn't know your druthers, so I got a variety."

"I'm not choosy." She picked up a snow pea pod with her chopsticks and nibbled at it. "Except when it comes to sharing my men."

"Men—is there more than one of us?" Max teased.

"How many women are you involved with?" she countered.

"One—and it's not Jenna, not Robin, nor anyone else you've conjured up. Why won't you trust me, Amy? What can I do to convince you I'm not the Casanova you've made me out to be?"

"It'll be difficult, considering there's always a group of females around eyeing you like you're the honey tree and they're a bunch of hungry bear cubs. Add into that the fact I've just spent an uncomfortable four hours trying to tend to business and at the same time, dodge you and your girlfriend."

"Which girlfriend? Since you seem to think I have so many."

"Jenna!" Amy snapped, too weary to control her temper. She jumped up from the table and started pacing the room, disgusted with herself over the outburst.

"I'm growing tired of defending myself," Max snapped back, grabbing Amy's arm and stopping her in her tracks. "Either you trust me or there's no future for us. Jenna isn't my girlfriend, she's—"

Amy's fingers on his lips silenced him. "Say no more," she said. Max was right. The issue was trust. Either she had to believe in him or forget him. "Let's enjoy the dinner you brought." She wanted the evening to be pleasant again.

Max apparently agreed, his ill humor vanishing as quickly as it had surfaced. As they ate, Max and Amy talked of this and that, the conversation flowing easily. They shared family stories and tales of their childhoods. She told him nostalgically of her visits with her grandparents at Torrence Place and he admitted to being a mischievous little boy, playing pranks on his sisters in typical brotherly fashion.

The glimpse into his past helped Amy realize how much she now *liked* Max, despite all her apprehensions. And liking for Amy was almost as essential an ingredient for a good life together as love itself was.

An hour later, the meal consumed, she strolled outside with him and the two sat on the steps of the gazebo. The night was pleasant, the humidity even tolerable. Max's glance went skyward. "Do you ever miss the stars?"

Amy looked up also. Only a smattering of lights could be seen in the heavens, typical of large cities where the reflection from the spangled skyline competed with Mother Nature. "Occasionally, but then I suppose I accept it as part of city life. Guess I appreciate the efficiency of freeways and malls enough to forgive the inconveniences."

"I'll have to take you to my ranch. From the patio, you can gaze up into eternity and discover that it sparkles like the incandescent offering of a billion fireflies."

"That's almost poetic. You—"

Amy's comment was lost when Max kissed her.

The kiss was like none other they'd shared. There was no tentativeness now. He seemed to sense her hunger, a hunger Amy was no longer able to suppress. She crushed herself against him as her arms went around him, her fingers caressing his soft dark hair. Passion flared so urgently Amy felt as radiant as those fictional fireflies. One kiss became two, then three, and Amy was lost in the marvel of his lovemaking.

"See how it can be between us," he said huskily, his labored breathing matching her own.

"That's what scares me. Passion isn't the same as love, Max."

"It's not a bad starting point," he murmured, helping Amy to her feet.

"But it isn't enough—for either one of us." Amy had to make Max understand.

He pulled her back into his arms, as though trying to persuade her otherwise with kisses. For a few moments, Amy gave in to him, savoring the intense feelings rocketing through her. *This has to end.* Then more resolutely, *Whoa, Amy.* She wriggled out of his arms, playfully fanning the air.

Max laughed. "Okay, you've gained another reprieve. You're about to use up your quota, though, pretty lady. One of these nights..."

Arms linking at their waists, Amy and Max walked inside and toward the front door. After long, lingering kisses in the foyer, Max whispered, "Let it happen, Amy. All you need to do is say 'yes.'" The door closed and he was gone.

Amy tarried there, more nonplussed than ever, her body tingling from the searing kisses and smothering embraces. As she switched the lamps off, only gravity kept her from floating to her quarters in the fashion of a lovesick cinematic heroine.

Then reality intruded once again. She wanted to trust Max—truly she did. Amy yearned to expel all feelings of skepticism and to revel in the magical night, rather than ruin it with introspection and suspicion.

But given Max's recent history, any intelligent woman, even one with token smarts, would avoid repetitions of tonight's brain-numbing lovemaking. Unfortunately, Amy's good sense was on holiday. She could hardly wait to be in Max's arms again.

When Amy returned from church at noon the next day, her answering machine was blinking with messages. There were three on the tape, an unusual number for a Sunday morning. All were from Jenna Peters.

Despite the implication of rudeness and her mother's lectures on manners running through her head, Amy delayed responding to the calls. To her way of thinking, she and Jenna had nothing to talk about.

When the telephone rang a few moments later, Amy let her machine take it, listening to see if it was Max or another call she should pick up. The person hung up without leaving a message. *Probably Jenna again*. No matter how insistent Max was about their not having a relationship, Jenna obviously had a different perception.

Amy changed into a black tank top and khaki shorts, then sat down to finish the huge Sunday edition of the *Chronicle*. She'd made her way to the Parade magazine section when the doorbell chimed.

Now who? Max? Amy slipped bare feet into her Birkenstock sandals and went expectantly to the foyer. Her hopes were dashed. Instead of Max, she was dumbfounded to see Jenna's distorted image through the thick leaded glass. *Talk about a woman with a mission*.

Jenna must be hell-bent on convincing an adversary that her man is spoken for.

Might as well get it over with. Amy would let Jenna have her say, be totally noncommittal, then speed her on her way before the lady knew what had hit her. She probably should have done this in the first place and spared herself a heap of turmoil. But Amy hadn't expected such persistence from one individual.

She also hadn't expected the hug Jenna wrapped her in when Amy opened the door.

"I'm so happy I could dance." Jenna twirled her in circles, making Amy so dizzy she collapsed on the foyer's brocade bench.

"Whoops!" Jenna extended a hand, assisting Amy to her feet. "Forgive my exuberance, but I thought this day would never happen. Now if you can only help me."

Her eyes were pleading and her tone so earnest that Amy didn't know how to react. Pushing her out the door no longer seemed an option. But what in heaven's name was all the giddiness about? "Why don't we go into the parlor and talk," Amy suggested.

"As soon as Max gets here."

"Max?" Amy felt the sensation one gets when an airplane unexpectedly hits an air pocket—a terrible clutch in the pit of her stomach.

"He's parking the car down the street." Jenna gestured to the line of cars in front of the house. "No available spaces nearby. Must be a party in the neighborhood."

Max then appeared in their line of vision and bounded up the steps. His expression was inscrutable. "Hello again," he said to Amy.

"Hello," she said, trying to hide her befuddlement. "I was just about to show Jenna into the parlor." She motioned for them to precede her and take a seat. "Would you both care for a cup of coffee?"

Jenna shook her head. "I'm really anxious to find out if you can do what I'm asking—or if you'll laugh in our faces when you discover why we're here."

Laughing was the farthest thing from Amy's mind right now. She felt uncomfortable, more so than she had when meeting with Max and Robin.

"I realize this is an imposition," Jenna said breathlessly, "and I promise I'll do everything I can to assist but...could you put together a wedding for Saturday? Money's not a problem."

Amy dropped onto a chair, her knees beginning to quiver. She wasn't about to be a collaborator to Max wedding another woman. Not this time. All the money in the world couldn't make her agree to such a preposterous request. If Jenna only knew what a rotten... Listen to yourself! You're getting absolutely paranoid. Trust, remember? Amy paused, assessing the situation.

Jenna had nothing to gain by deliberately going out of her way to hurt her. And Max, Max would never be so cruel. Last night he'd assured her he was sincere in his courtship, that he wasn't stringing her along.

However, that didn't explain why he was here with Jenna. Nor did it make arranging a wedding in a matter of days doable. "*This* Saturday? No way."

Jenna bit her lip and looked toward Max for support.

"I know it's kind of impulsive," he said, "but impulsiveness seems to be a fatal flaw in our family."

"Family?"

Max nodded. "Jenna is my favorite cousin." He halted momentarily, allowing time for his remark to sink in before saying, "Now why don't I make that coffee? We could all use a cup while you and Jenna hash things out."

Amy shot him a sharp glance as he left the room, sorry that a glance was her only weapon of retaliation. *Cousin indeed*. She could have gleefully throttled the man. He who once accused her of jealousy had done all he could to foster it—and succeeded. Dazedly she prompted Jenna to go on. "Perhaps you'd better—"

"Of course," Jenna burbled. "You see I've been in love with Jack Denning since high school. We planned to marry right after we finished college and Jack got his wings. He's a navy pilot. Anyway, just when everything was about to materialize, we had a silly argument and our engagement was broken. Now fate has brought us back together and we want to share every second we can.

"Jack's stationed on an aircraft carrier in the Mediterranean and has leave coming up. Next week. Leave we're going to use for a wedding and a honeymoon in Italy. That's why the date's not negotiable."

"So what is Max's role? And why is he tagging along now?"

"He's the one who gave fate a hand and told me to go for it. A total reversal of the jaded tune he sang when Jack and I split. His position then was something to the effect that 'there are always other fish in the sea—other fly-boy sailors, too.' But that was before Max met you. Lately he's become a regular matchmaker."

Amy felt a brief surge of euphoria. If Max was encouraging other lovers...

"Back to the wedding." Jenna took Amy's hand. "I wanted to talk yesterday about the possibility of your helping us, but you were so busy I couldn't corral you. In fact, I almost got the impression you were avoiding me, doubly so when you didn't return my phone calls. That's why I insisted Max drive me over here today—I wanted to ensure you'd see me."

When Amy offered no response or denial, Jenna continued, "Please say you'll do this for me. Please have this weekend free. Don't tell me Torrence Place is booked."

"No, it's not. Still I've never put together a wedding so hastily. It may not be possible."

"Anything's possible. Jack and I reconciling has convinced me of that."

"But *here*? To your set, Torrence Place is poison."

"Ridiculous. It's a beautiful house, just right for us. I knew the minute I saw it. Anyway, I don't care what others think. Maybe my wedding will dispel any rumors of a hex."

"What about invitations?"

"Too late for those. I'll call everyone. It'll only be a small gathering—mostly family and very close friends."

"I take it you've talked her into doing the wedding," Max said to Jenna as he entered the room carrying three mugs. "I told you she's a sucker for romance." He grinned.

"Don't get too comfortable," Amy warned Max. "I'm not through with you yet." But she was smiling on the inside.

"So where do we begin?" Jenna's bubbly enthusiasm filled the room, enveloping everything, including Amy. It was infectious. Amy found herself getting emotional at the woman's joy. She also was counting the minutes until she could speak to Max alone and could give him an earful.

When the phone rang shortly after Jenna and Max left, Amy grabbed it. It was Max. "Why didn't you tell me she was a relative?" Amy demanded before he could say more than hello.

"Realizing you'd jumped to the wrong conclusion, I found jerking your chain irresistible. Then I began to comprehend that your anger revealed more than you were admitting. It said you cared."

"So maybe I cared. But when were you going to tell me about Jenna?"

"I was going to last night—"

Amy remembered that she was the one who'd called a halt to his explanations. "I'm beginning to figure out how demoniac you can be," she grumbled, trying to cover up her humor. "Coming over here with her and letting me think...all kinds of things."

"Jenna asked me to come and I couldn't turn her down. Besides, you asked for it. Accusing me of chasing after enough females to exhaust an Olympian. Keeping my proposal hanging." Amy could envision the impish grin accompanying his words.

"So has your faith in the institution of marriage been restored?" Max asked.

"My faith wasn't gone—just a little shaken," she retorted.

Max laughed. "If you want, we could make it a double wedding. I'm sure Jenna wouldn't mind."

"There's no way I'd steal another woman's thunder on her wedding day."

"So I'll have to come over and wear down your resistance," Max said, disconnecting the phone before Amy could argue.

She rolled her eyes. What was she going to do with Max? Once he set his mind to something, there appeared to be no way of changing it. *So why then had he let Robin slip away*? Amy finally dared to believe it was partly because of her.

Max arrived within the hour, carrying a picnic basket of gourmet goodies and a bottle of vintage wine. Amy had catered enough events to know the repast cost several hundred dollars. Not exactly the Sunday afternoon leftovers she was used to.

"Is this to wear me down or to assuage your guilt?" she gibed.

"Neither," Max returned. "It's to say thanks for doing Jenna's wedding. And for not holding my little prank against me. I knew you couldn't keep withstanding my charm."

"Typical egotistical male. Until you showed up with Jenna today, I'd forgotten all about you."

Max kissed her nose. "Aren't you afraid telling such fibs will make it grow long, like Pinocchio's? Face it, there's no way you could have dismissed what happened between us last night. I know I haven't been able to stop thinking about it."

She didn't answer.

"You're still a little cross. I believe I have the treatment for that." Max took the wine and began uncorking the bottle.

"I'm not cross, but I am discovering all your bad habits—like being a merciless tease and popping surprises. I've had enough of your torment, Max."

"No more...torment...then." He put down the wine and moved closer to her.

"You're twisting my words. When I said torment, I was talking about the way you purposely misled me about Jenna, the way you make sport of marriage with impulsive proposals. And don't feed me that stuff about it being a 'family flaw.'"

"My family has another flaw—going after what we want." He laced his fingers with hers. "I'm sorry for causing you to think I'm not sincere about marriage. I am, absolutely. I've told you repeatedly what I want. *I want you to be my wife.*"

"Oh, right," she scoffed, secretly pleased, but not wanting to make things too easy for him. She was beginning to enjoy the repartee. "I'm the flavor of the week. What about all the weeks to come—will you be as certain once the novelty wears off?"

"You're a gigantic fraud, Amy Holt." He pressed their joined hands against his chest.

"And why is that?"

"All this romance jazz, 'love forever after,' blah blah blah...yet when a man comes along offering precisely that, you can't accept it."

"That's not true. No one—" She caught herself. Did he say "love" and "forever after"? The words dangled like a beautiful lure and Amy knew she was hooked.

Over the next week, Amy's reluctance vanished with an onslaught of official courtship. During the day, she worked frantically on the myriad details of Jenna's wedding. Evenings, however, were reserved for Max. They went to movies, saw a touring Broadway musical, and he treated her to dinner at various restaurants, from the exclusive Café Annie to trendy neighborhood spots in the Montrose area.

At first Amy was concerned about encountering a society reporter and reviving the unwanted publicity. Then she relaxed. So someone saw them together and told the world they were a couple? Amy was almost ready to shout it from the rooftops and say "consequences be damned."

Whenever fears over Max's reasons for pursuing her arose, Amy rapidly subdued them. It was pointless to keep on searching for ulterior motives. The media glare was over and business at "Arrangements by Amy" was booming. Both she and Max had recovered from the devastation caused by his canceled wedding. Now they were together because they wanted to be.

It was raining the morning of Jenna's wedding. Not just a sprinkle, but a raging downpour. Amy looked out to see water gushing in currents along the curbs. She groaned. But Jenna's and Jack's laughter as they arrived toting oversize umbrellas reassured her. A hurricane could be churning in the Gulf and they wouldn't fuss. Amy might not be able to erase all her tension about something going wrong with the wedding, but at least she wouldn't have to fret about the principals failing to show at the appointed hour.

The white folding chairs in the parlor were filled with guests when the pianist's fanfare signaled the ceremony's start and Jenna slowly descended the staircase toward the trellised archway where Jack waited. From her spot at the end of the hallway, Amy had full view of the procession, but rather than watching the bride, her eyes were on Max just as his were fixed on her. All week he'd kidded her about a double wedding and right now Amy wished she were the one standing at that improvised altar, with him at her side.

As she witnessed the age-old vows, Amy made a decision. Max had asked her to marry him repeatedly. Tonight, once the guests were gone and they were alone, she would tell him yes. Perhaps she was unduly influenced by the beautiful ceremony or the radiant faces of Jack and Jenna. Yet Amy knew there was more to it than that.

The simple truth was she loved Max and saw no value in waiting. So people might talk at the speed with which they'd gotten together. She no longer dreaded such scuttlebutt. As Max had once intimated, there were no timetables to falling in love. No explanation for it, either.

Love was a wonderful mystery. Who should know that better than Amy, who'd made a career of romance?

When the piano erupted in music and photographers began snapping the bride and groom, Amy remembered her duties and sent the maids passing through the crowd with trays of champagne-filled flutes while Stephanie supervised the food table. Satisfied that all services were moving smoothly, Amy hurried to the kitchen to check on things there. Max came up behind her, folding her in his arms and covering her neck with warm quick kisses. She spun around to face him and responded unhesitatingly to a more passionate kiss.

"I wish that had been us getting married," he murmured, echoing her earlier thoughts.

"Perhaps it can be."

"Do you mean—"

"Later," Amy whispered, kissing him once more before rushing off to attend to the reception.

The shuffle of windup activities was over. Amy and Max were sitting side by side in the solarium holding hands and sipping the remains of a bottle of champagne. His dinner jacket hung over the back of a chair along with his tie. Likewise, Amy'd removed her shoes and kicked them under a table. Jenna and Jack, ensconced in the Hearts and Flowers Suite upstairs, had finally gotten their long-awaited privacy. The house had a wonderful quietness to it.

Amy loved the transformation that had come over Max. For so long, he'd proudly worn the mantle of a doubting Thomas, a caustic naysayer to the glories of love; now he'd become tender and sentimental.

Tracing a finger around the rim of his glass, he said with a refreshing modesty, "I can hardly believe you've agreed to be my wife." He set the glass down and settled her into his lap. "I adore you."

A tiny cough interrupted their embrace. It was Jenna, still in her wedding dress.

Amy jumped to her feet. "Is something wrong with the suite?"

"No," Jenna said, her cheeks turning a pinker shade despite the fact all her makeup was gone. Kissed off, no doubt. "This is so... could you help me a second?"

Reluctantly Amy followed Jenna to the Bride's Room. Jenna explained, "The zipper on my dress is stuck and I can't get it undone. Jack couldn't do it either. Can you? Use scissors if necessary."

Amy smiled. "Let me have a go at it, and if that doesn't work, I'll get the scissors." As Amy slowly maneuvered the zipper of the white lace sheath, up a little, down a little, Jenna prattled on, probably to cover her embarrassment. All it took was a bit of patience, something of which Jack understandably had none, and the zipper was unstuck. Regrettably, during Jenna's nonstop monologue, Amy'd heard more than she wanted to about Max. When she returned downstairs, the tender mood that had prevailed earlier was replaced by a seething rage.

Max reached out his arms to her, but she stayed her ground, glaring down at him. "Do you really love me so much, or do you have other incentives for rushing to the altar?"

"What are you talking about?"

"I've been talking to Jenna."

"And?"

"I've finally found out why you're so anxious to take a bride."

CHAPTER TEN

"I'M AFRAID you've lost me." Max rubbed his chin, now shadowed by a faint stubble of beard. "I thought we'd come to an understanding. Suddenly you're back to that old grievance that I'm desperate for a wife."

"'Desperate' wasn't what I said."

"Desperate...anxious. Same difference," he snapped, rising to his feet. "What precisely is on your mind?"

"Jenna told me about securing her inheritance," Amy answered. "About your grandfather Barstow and his stipulations."

"Oh?"

"Yes, she informs me that only *married* heirs are eligible to share in your grandfather's fortune."

"I see." Max paused before continuing. "So after a thorough analysis, you've concluded that my proposal to you is tied in with the legacy?" One eyebrow was raised derisively.

"We both know how important money is to you. You're constantly harping about mine."

Max's expression grew dark and his voice gave evidence of a fury that had been stoked like the engines of an old fire-eating locomotive. "You little idiot! You seriously think some piddling inheritance is driving me toward the altar?"

"Lots of people have married for such reasons," Amy said defiantly. The Evans clan might have more money than Croesus, but Max worked hard at generating even more and there were numerous indications to prove her case that the almighty dollar mattered to him. Not only the frequent comments about her finances and the investment crisis in Dallas prematurely rousting him out of hiding, but choosing Robin. Max had never acknowledged as much, but Amy suspected that part of Robin's appeal rested with her not needing his bankroll.

People with assets aplenty were often strapped when it came to liquidity; marrying her now and gaining the inheritance might be the most expedient way to secure ready cash. He hadn't shared that much about Evans Enterprises. For all Amy knew, an exciting new project beckoned and he needed some fast money.

Max stood statue-still, hands braced on hips. His eyes, however, were shooting sparks. "Boy, you're one piece of work. Just when I thought I'd finally convinced you of my sincerity, you come up with this. Apparently you're unconvinceable. If your indictment wasn't so insulting, I'd laugh. But frankly I'm too teed off to find any humor here.

"Can't you believe someone could want you just for you? No, you're so damn suspicious—" Max threw a hand in the air. "For the record, I don't *need* a wife. For a while there, I *thought* I wanted one. Apparently, another lapse of judgment on my part, one of many I seem to be having lately.

"I promise you, though, it's a lapse that won't happen again. I haven't had one calm moment since the idea of marriage entered my head. Thanks for sparing me any more trauma." With that he stormed off toward the door.

Amy remained fixed in place, speechless in the face of Max's vitriolic lecture and theatrical exit. A minute later, gathering her wits, she noticed his tie and jacket hanging on the chair. She followed his route to the hall in an attempt to catch up with him, but Max had left. The grandfather clock was chiming twelve. How fitting, Amy reflected bitterly. Prince Charming was gone from her life, and Cinderella was about to turn back into a drudge.

The newlyweds departed early and Amy spent the rest of Sunday preparing for the first of the retreats. Stephanie had requested the day off, so Amy was deprived of her assistance and her advice. She was deprived, too, of full concentration, distracted as she was by flashbacks to last night. Nothing could prevent the incident from playing and replaying in her head.

The more she pondered the conversation with Jenna, and Max's indignant response, the more Amy nursed a rising dread she'd misinterpreted the situation. She should have quizzed Jenna more before tearing into Max. It didn't seem logical for him to be so irate if Amy's charges were close to the mark.

Okay, maybe he did care for her a bit, but Amy couldn't accept those denials about the money being completely unimportant. "Piddling" was how he'd described his grandfather's legacy. Only a million or two perhaps?

She'd been hoping for too much, Amy conceded. True romance must be the stuff of fiction, not real people. *No, that's not always the case. Jenna and Jack have that kind of love, so do Steph and Jay, Eva and Ralph, my parents, and loads of others I could name. To settle for less would be just that... settling.* Why then did she feel like her insides were being ripped to shreds?

The debate wrested her one way, then another. If she had overreacted, there was no subtle way to find out the truth. Jenna was off on her honeymoon in Italy and wouldn't return to Houston for a week.

Her only recourse was to call Max. He might chew on her some more, or refuse to talk at all, but taking the initiative was her sole alternative so she'd grit her teeth and do it. If she'd misconstrued the issue of the legacy, she'd apologize... grovel if necessary.

"Evans."

"Hello, Max. It's me."

"Yes?" An arctic voice.

He's still very angry. Amy shouldn't have been surprised. She'd been out of line to reproach him before hearing his side of the story. "I wanted to let you know I'm feeling bad about last night."

"I see. You hurl all sorts of ulterior motives at me, label me a mercenary, and now want absolution?"

"Well, no..." Max certainly wasn't making this easy. "I simply wanted to... that is, I... I thought maybe you could come over." Hopefully, Max would be more amenable to discussing this misunderstanding in person. As it stood, there was little chance of penetrating that closed mind of his over the phone.

"What for?"

"Must I justify my request?"

Silence from Max.

Apparently she must. "You left your dinner jacket here."

"I see. You're not responsible for articles left over twenty-four hours—is that it?"

"Of course not. I—"

"I'll send someone for it. Goodbye." The click of his receiver sounded in her ear.

He'd send someone. She could tell from his tone that Max wasn't going to budge an inch. But anyone could make a mistake, including her. Just because she'd acted badly didn't mean Max shouldn't give her another chance. Especially if he loved her as much as he claimed. In all fairness, Amy had to admit that her presumptions weren't very loving, either. At least she felt ashamed and wanted to make amends. That should count for something.

When darkness fell, Amy gave up hearing from Max that night. She was preparing for bed when the doorbell rang. Hoping against hope that he'd changed his mind, she reached for her robe. Her emotions ran the gamut from excitement to panic as she raced toward the entry to answer the bell.

"Hello," she said, opening the door. "Come in."

"I'll stay out here. My jacket? That was the excuse for your call, wasn't it?"

"You made it apparent I needed an excuse. Please come in. We have to talk."

"As I recall, you did a significant amount of talking yesterday."

"I was wrong." Even though Max had provided no clarification, Amy was now positive she'd misjudged him. Loving Max—which she now knew she did—meant it was time to start demonstrating it.

"What made you decide that?"

"Trust," she answered breathlessly. "Faith in you."

"A bit late in surfacing, wouldn't you say?"

"Listen—" Her hackles were rising. "I'm trying to tell you I don't give a darn about that endowment and I regret what I said. I want us to be friends again."

"Pardon me if I don't jump through hoops over your wants," he said sourly.

"Why are you being so disagreeable?"

"You want me agreeable?" He swept her inside and pushed the door closed behind them, trapping her up against it, crushing his lips against hers.

Amy wanted his kiss, but a kiss of love, not this punishment. She shoved against him and Max immediately broke the embrace.

"No?" he asked.

"No. Not when you have such animosity."

"Whatever you wish." He held his hands up in a no-touch gesture.

"What I wish is for us to talk about this," Amy said emphatically. "To—"

"I'm sick to death of talking. I asked one thing from you, Amy—for you to believe in me... I suppose that was too much to expect. I don't care to spend the rest of my life wondering what transgression I'll be hit with next." He retrieved his jacket from the coat tree.

Tears of hurt rolled down Amy's cheeks as she watched him bound down the steps and into the night.

"Thank God," Stephanie exclaimed the next afternoon as she collapsed into a kitchen chair and slipped off her shoes. "One day down and four to go. I never dreamed hosting meetings would be so demanding. With private-duty nursing I do get to sit down occasionally."

"They were a bit taxing," Amy agreed, joining Stephanie at the table and also shedding her shoes.

"By the way, did you notice that hunky lawyer in the group today?" Stephanie asked. Obviously attributing Amy's red-ringed eyes that morning to Max, Stephanie had spent the entire day trying to perk her up. Leave it to Steph to latch on to a surrogate male for Amy as the best way to accomplish that.

"Speaking of hunky men, Steph, I believe I heard yours arriving." It was the ideal way for Amy to extricate herself from the unwanted discussion, as Stephanie grabbed her shoes and ran out to greet Jay. Amy had to stifle a twitch of envy. Must be wonderful, she thought, to be in a relationship like theirs.

The next four days were repeats of Monday: cooking, cleaning, nonstop pleasantries and total exhaustion at the end of the day. These retreats had convinced Amy that weddings were her cup of tea, not corporate functions. The job satisfaction just wasn't the same. Finally the last session was over.

"I never thought I'd be relieved we don't have a wedding scheduled," Stephanie said, "but I'm ready for some major solitude this weekend." Stephanie was standing at the back door, her hand pushing the screen open.

"Jay's working?" Amy asked.

"Not *that* much solitude, silly. What about you? What are you up to?"

"Staying home," she told Stephanie defensively, "and counting my money."

"You and Scrooge McDuck. This has been some turnaround, hasn't it? Like a miracle." Stephanie didn't wait for an answer. Instead she scooted on out. Stephanie was right, the reversal of fortune had been a miracle.

Even before the trouble with Max and Robin, Amy had been living close to the edge, but now she had more business than she and Stephanie could handle. Amy had already rehired the cleaning service, and was considering a part-time secretary. Just this week, she'd signed four new contracts, three for business seminars and one for a December wedding.

Saturday was lonely. Amy tried to pass the hours by inspecting the area upstairs. Besides the Hearts and Flowers Suite and the Bride's Room, there were three other bedrooms and a hallway bath, the latter yet to be renovated. She should be able to afford redoing one more bedroom and the bathroom, then next year, if business continued improving, finish out the other two bedrooms. They would be perfect for— Amy bit her lip. Torrence Place was designed for children, for a family, just as it had been in her grandparents' day.

Would those rooms ever be filled with children? Not unless she stopped picturing little boys who resembled Max Evans. She hadn't heard from him since their falling-out, but once again Max was making the news. This time the media attention involved a partnership he was forming with some Mexico City developers.

By noon, Amy couldn't stand it any longer; she had to get out. She'd visit some antique shops on West Nineteenth, a few blocks away. If she saw something appropriate for the new bedroom, she might go ahead and buy it.

Hours later, she emerged from the last shop, delighted with her finds—nothing for the bedroom, but a mint-condition Royal Vienna chocolate set and, from a vintage clothing store, a turn-of-the-century wedding gown. The gown was Amy's size and in good condition. But she wasn't buying it to wear. The dress would become a wall decoration for the Bride's Room.

Once home, she dusted off the chocolate set and found a place for it in the parlor, then sat there studying the four walls. What to do now? She was still lonely—she missed Max.

Sunday was more wretched than the day before. Amy tried to start the day off on a positive note by attending church. That occupied only the morning. She watched TV, rifled through the Sunday paper, paid her bills, and brooded a lot. When the phone rang at four, Amy desperately grabbed at it.

It was Jenna. Jack's leave was over and he had just departed for his duty station. "Can you stand to have dinner with a weepy newlywed?"

Amy eagerly agreed to go, thinking that misery does indeed love company. Even though their states of misery had different bases, she and Jenna were in the same boat—the SS Pitiful. They settled on a new pasta restaurant near the Galleria.

"Shall I phone Max and ask him to join us?"

"Not a good idea. Max and I are not even on speaking terms at the moment." Amy sighed mournfully. Jenna's mention of Max had loosened her fragile grip on her emotions.

"What's the problem?"

"It's too complicated to go into on the phone," Amy stalled. *I want to know about Robin...the break-up...about the inheritance. I deserve a few answers for all I've been through.* "We'll talk at the restaurant. See you at seven."

When she saw Amy arrive, Jenna waved from a high-backed booth near the rear of the restaurant, then rose for an exchange of hugs. As Amy turned to sit down, her eyes met Max's. "What's *he* doing here?"

"I might ask the same thing," Max said irritably. "My cousin lured me out with a sob story about being distressed over Jack's leaving. Now that I see what's up, I think I'll be leaving myself."

"Oh, no, you don't," Jenna protested. "If you value my feelings at all, you'll stay put."

"How do *your* feelings come into play here?"

"Remorse, that's how. This mess between you two is all my fault." She turned to Amy. "After I talked to you, it was pretty clear I wasn't the only one feeling distressed right now," Jenna explained. "So I called Max and he filled in the gaps. The way I see it, my tale about the family legacy stirred up a hornet's nest. Right?"

"Sort of. But you're not totally liable," Amy assured her. "My thinking was skewed."

She glanced over at Max. He seemed more absorbed in the menu than in her conciliatory comments. Her temper flared as she raised her voice to attract his attention. "But who can blame me for being mixed-up after all that's transpired recently?"

Max's response was a weighty sigh.

"So," Amy went on, "after you told me about Grandfather Barstow's conditions..."

"You put two and two together," Jenna said.

Amy nodded. "And got five."

Jenna looked to the ceiling, as though searching for divine inspiration. "How stupid of me. I should have never brought it up."

"Amy's deduction was all her own doing," Max broke in.

"It seemed plausible, considering how much you covet money," Amy fired back.

Max gave her a gimlet-eyed stare. "Working damn hard to be successful isn't exactly the same as coveting money. I can struggle along without the boon of Gramps's fortune."

"Now, now," Jenna reproached. "You probably didn't bother to enlighten Amy with the whole story, did you, Max?"

"I never got the opportunity," he growled, snapping a bread stick in half.

"Puhleasssse," Amy countered. "I wanted to hear you out, practically prostrated myself at your feet, but you clammed up. How long is this surly mood to go on?"

"Pax! Both of you!" Jenna rested her elbows on the table and leaned in toward Amy. "Great-Great-Grandfather Barstow's will has been a family joke for years. Everyone who marries gets congratulatory cards on their big windfall—actually a thousand dollars each, not much money in this day and age. What's so funny to all of us is that what Gramps wanted and what he got are so far apart.

"He was trying to ensure that his name lived on when he stipulated that every descendent—once married—was entitled to the inheritance. Unfortunately for the old man, none of the males in the line produced sons. So much for trying to bribe your way into immortality. The Barstow name died out long ago, but the legacy survives.

"And when you decided that Max—" Jenna giggled. "What a hoot. A new story to add to the legend."

"One which better not come up when I'm around," Max ordered. "Now if you two will pardon me, I'm sure you'll have a much better evening without my 'surly' company."

Amy stood so he could get out. "Don't go away mad," she called as Max disappeared with little more than a nod. "Just go away period," she muttered.

"Cut him a bit of slack," Jenna soothed as Amy slumped dejectedly back down into the booth.

"Lot of good that will do. It's becoming perfectly plain that Max and I were never meant for each other. Better that it ended now."

"This isn't the end. Max is in love," Jenna said, smiling knowingly. "So are you."

"Your cousin doesn't have the faintest notion what love is. He told me once about his lack of faith in it. I should have believed him then and saved myself all this anguish."

"Like I said, cut him a bit of slack. Max is a confused man. He's always been so self-assured and now he's completely discombobulated."

"I won't argue that point," Amy said, looking up at the advancing waiter who took their orders and left. She decided to use this break in the conversation to ask all those unanswered questions, salvage what she could of this unsettling evening. "About Robin...how could he have even considered marrying someone like her?"

"Actually, she's not all bad, mostly terribly spoiled. I knew from Max's attitude that it wasn't the romance of the century, but they were compatible and fun to be with. Most of Max's friends and family were pleased when they became engaged."

"Including you?" Amy asked.

"Yeah." Jenna shrugged. "What can I say? We didn't know her as well as we supposed. Once she had that ring on her finger, though, her true colors began to show. I think it was when Max insisted on the small wedding that the transformation began. You see, Robin was a darling as long as she was getting her way and, for the most part, when they were dating, Max let her have her way."

"So I simply entered the picture at an inopportune moment?"

"Actually at the most opportune moment. Robin was being a stinker and Max was already having second thoughts. Then he met you and was thrown for a loop."

"He told you that?"

Jenna sipped her drink. "Not in so many words, but he didn't have to. I've known him too long and too well not to see something in him that had never been there before. From those first meetings with you, he was intrigued. I doubt he realized what was occurring at the start, or knew how his eyes sort of lit up when he mentioned you."

"I couldn't tell."

"Naturally. Max is an honorable guy and he was engaged to another woman. In his mind, a binding commitment had been made. Then Robin pulled that late arrival stunt, behaving as if the wedding were no more important than the opening of a new carwash, and he just lost it. Read her the riot act and she retorted that he could 'stuff it' or something equally ladylike. So they broke up."

"How do you know all this?"

"Robin. She shared chapter and verse. Max isn't the type of guy to blab. But he did tell me he had no regrets. It didn't take any sleuthing to conclude it was because he'd met you."

"Maybe," Amy admitted. "But that still doesn't explain his haste—"

"Max is a man of action. He wanted you and once free, he went after you. But you've been difficult to catch, a rare experience for Max. Then you go and accuse him of wanting you merely to get his hands on—" Jenna started giggling again. "He's reeling."

Rather nice to have him reeling instead of me. "Supposing everything you say is on the mark, what do you suggest I do?"

"Give it a few days. Max will come around, I promise. If he doesn't, then you could..." For the rest of the evening, Jenna advised Amy on various ways to win Max over. In Jenna's view, Amy and Max were a solid love match, destined to be together. Nothing like a newlywed spouting the wonderments of love and trying to convert everyone in her path.

In spite of Jenna's optimism, Amy felt only despair. First, it was unlikely Max would ever swallow his pride and forgive her. Second, there was no way she would carry through with any of Jenna's suggestions. No matter how much it hurt, Amy was going to have to accept the fact she'd run Max off for good.

CHAPTER ELEVEN

HER conviction that Max wouldn't change his mind about reconciling had little effect on Amy's reactions during the next week. Each time the telephone or doorbell rang, she raced to answer like a sprinter in a track meet. She watched every newscast and searched the papers daily for a mention of Max or Evans Enterprises, but was doomed to disappointment in all cases. He seemed to have dropped off the face of the earth.

By Friday, distraught and embarrassed over her obsession, Amy knew she must get her life back on an even keel. Tonight she'd go to a movie, have dinner somewhere. If Stephanie was busy, she'd find someone else to go with.

Might have known he'd pick this particular night to make his move, Amy grumbled when she arrived home from the movie to find Max's taped message. "I've been away all week . . . spending most of that time thinking about you instead of the business at hand. Have dinner with me . . . I promise I'll be more rational." A longer pause, then he added, "If *you* will."

Amy didn't know what to do. She wanted to dial him back as fast as she could push the buttons. On the other hand, he'd left her in limbo for five days—five whole days. So he'd had a business trip. So what? He could have called.

With the advent of cellular telephones, there was no such thing as being out of touch. If he'd traveled by plane, train, ship, car or snowmobile, he could have called. If he'd walked to wherever he'd gone, he could have called. But he hadn't.

Amy fully intended to talk to Max, but not the second he'd snapped his fingers. "Today's Friday..." she mentally counted "...next Wednesday should be about right."

"Thor Offshore Drilling Corporation?" Stephanie was setting up the breakfast buffet on Monday while Amy filled the electric coffee urn with water. "Never heard of them."

"Me neither. But after thumbing through this directory from the chamber of commerce, I realized there must be hundreds of businesses in Houston we've never heard of. All of them potential clients." She plugged in the coffee maker and went to pour the orange juice.

Tables were lined up according to Thor specifications, flip charts in place and an overhead projector at the ready when members of the new group filtered in. In need of more assistance today, Amy had a college student answering the door and handing out packets.

Amy was placing a freshly baked apple coffeecake on the buffet table when she felt a tap on the shoulder. She glanced up and saw it was the company comptroller. Removing her insulated mitts, Amy turned to greet him.

"Ms. Holt, have you met our CEO?"

Amy was too flabbergasted to immediately speak. She stood numbly as the comptroller introduced her to Max Evans.

"Mr. Evans," Amy managed, keeping her acknowledgment detached, purposefully setting the tone for any subsequent encounters between them. Max was more devious than she'd given him credit for, catching her off guard like this. "Welcome again to Torrence Place. Let me know if there's anything we can do for you and please tell everyone to help themselves." She gestured toward the food, then swiftly moved from the table into the kitchen, hoping she could suppress the overwhelming urge to cry. The shock of seeing Max again was almost too much to bear.

He followed after her. "Amy—"

"I'm sorry but I'm extremely busy right now." She took a tray from under the counter and filled it with glasses of juice.

"But you asked whether there was anything you could do for me. I can think of all number of things..." He ran a hand down her arm, distracting Amy further and causing her to tip a glass over.

"Look what you've made me do," she fussed, grabbing a cloth to mop up the sticky mess.

"If you'd only listen—"

Max was interrupted by the approach of one of his vice presidents seeking advice on a scheduling mix-up and, in the process, earning Amy's appreciation. She needed a chance to adjust to Max's being here. Her relief was doubled when the two men wandered out of the kitchen and into the solarium where the meeting was to take place.

If she'd known of Max's association with this company, Amy would have told them—politely, of course—what they could do with their business. She was no masochist. To knowingly put herself in Max's presence for two days would be akin to self-flagellation. Her heart would never begin healing if he was constantly underfoot.

Nevertheless, she was thrilled to see him, yet also determined that Max would not discover just how thrilled. He wasn't going to get a scrap of her attention during these meetings.

So that's how it's going to be. Max had attempted to speak with Amy all morning and she'd rebuffed every overture. She might *try* to ignore him, but Max had no intention of allowing the snubs to continue.

"The pencils need sharpening." It was midmorning and Max had tracked Amy to her office. He stood at her elbow, his breath warm in her ear, his hand clutching a box of new pencils.

"What?"

"A hearing disorder, Ms. Holt? I said the pencils need sharpening. It's not complicated. You find a sharpener, insert them and voilà! They're much more useful with points." His eyes glinted devilishly.

"I'll get right on those pencils, *Mr*. Evans." Max could tell she was speaking through clenched teeth and the rosy color of her cheeks said she wasn't as indifferent to his attentions as she'd been trying to pretend. By now, Max knew Amy like a book—that revealing blush he was glimpsing, her quick temper when she felt wronged, the protective barriers she threw up each time he drew near. He was going to use that temper of hers to his advantage by poking and prodding until it sizzled.

He almost felt guilty over his next words. Almost, but not quite. "Before you do the pencils, would you check on the coffee? It's so weak a baby could drink it. Trying to cut corners on expenses?" That had to get to her. Amy's coffee was perfect—she probably made the best coffee in Houston.

As he'd expected, Amy snapped at the bait. "Do you enjoy pestering me?" She glared at him. "What's going to be your next complaint—that the orange juice is too pulpy?"

Max grinned. "Nope, the orange juice is fine. The only problem is the coffee. Oh, and the pencils, of course."

"If you knew what's good for you, you'd be glad the pencils are dull. A sane man would avoid equipping me with anything sharp right now." Thankfully, they were alone with no witnesses in hearing distance. Amy heaved a sigh. She couldn't continue to vent her frustrations like this—not in a business environment.

However, once he'd provoked that reaction, Max let up. He'd gotten what he wanted; he didn't want Amy furious. He was just tired of being slighted. At the noon recess, he'd apologize and invite her to dinner. Then maybe they could pick up where they'd left off.

"Dinner? You have the nerve to ask me to waste another hour with you when I've spent the morning making enough trips between the kitchen and solarium to wear a path in the flooring? No way."

Okay, lady. Apparently the morning didn't do it. If you think I've been obnoxious so far, just wait and see what else I can dish out.

Max glanced gleefully at the dining table with its sparkling crystal, china and silver, all readied for an elegant sit-down meal as Amy announced, "Please be seated and we'll serve lunch."

"Hold on, gang," Max broke in, "we're running way behind." He turned to Amy. "Would you mind serving us while we work?"

She minded, just as Max knew she would. The flame in those dark eyes said Amy would like to dump the meal over his head. Max realized he wouldn't care. It might be messy, but at least it would alleviate the tension between them. Then he could kiss her silly and... *Better not think about kissing her anymore if I want to make it through the rest of this meeting.*

As she stewed in the kitchen, Amy concluded that Max hadn't spent a single moment doing whatever a CEO was supposed to do at these events. He'd been too busy inventing ways of getting under her skin to have accomplished any real work. Replacing another of her prized Lenox Rose china plates in the pantry, Amy said a blessing that she'd controlled the impulse to sail one at Max's head.

There was no way she could endure more of his aggravation today. She wasn't one of those minions who had to bow and scrape to the big boss. Let him abuse them for a while. That settled, Amy asked Stephanie to take charge, then escaped upstairs.

"He's gone," Steph assured her a few hours later when she found Amy tidying a linen cupboard.

"Don't say anything else," Amy threatened, glimpsing Stephanie's smirk. Max's shenanigans had her feeling like the recipient of a battering ram and she wasn't up to any of her associate's well-meaning platitudes. There was no comfort in the fact the workday was over and everyone was gone. Max would be back tomorrow, even better armed.

As she thought about Max's behavior, the harassment, the demands, she slowly began to comprehend that he was yanking her chain just as he'd done about Jenna. And she, twice the fool, was yanking back, causing grief only to herself. Well, it was time to even the score. Tomorrow's round would belong to her.

For Tuesday's session, Amy tripled the amount of coffee grounds so that the final brew resembled India ink. Volley number one. When she saw Max walking toward the urn, Amy waited patiently for him to press the spigot and take a sip. *Yes*! she congratulated, as the movement of his throat gave evidence of his struggle to fight back a grimace. When Max's eyes caught hers across the room, Amy feigned the most innocent of expressions. He boldly took another swallow, then saluted her with the cup. *Hell's bells. Max never behaved as anticipated.*

The pencils were sharpened and she'd had Stephanie and the student helper taste-test the orange juice, since she'd stupidly offered it to him as a target. Not a single disparaging word came from his lips. Amy wondered whether Max would gripe if all the pencil points were broken and the orange juice was full of seeds. He was being the epitome of courtesy and goodwill. Reverse psychology, she suspected.

But just in case, she'd planned a simple lunch of pasta salad and sandwiches—a menu that would travel just fine no matter where Max chose to eat, even in the park up the street. Score two for her side.

Her triumph lasted only until the group began trooping out the front door toward the Thor limos. On their way, according to Max, to a nearby restaurant. Amy counted to ten—she hadn't bested him at all. He was just biding his time before letting go with today's zinger.

"A treat for my staff," he proclaimed proudly. "We've gotten so much done I decided they deserved a reward."

"If you were planning this, why didn't you tell me sooner and save me the work and the money?"

"Perhaps I should have." His regret was unconvincing. "Let me make it up to you—why don't you and Stephanie come along?"

"Can't. I'll be too busy packing away the leftover food. But I'm sure Stephanie would like to go."

"Your choice," he said. "See you at two."

She carefully cartoned the salad and bagged the sandwiches. They would be lunch for weeks until she gagged on the monotony. Speaking of gagging, she'd like to... *You're doing it again. Letting Max frazzle you. And for no good reason.*

The more she reflected on Max's antics, the more Amy realized what they really signaled. He meant no harm, just the opposite. Only a man who cared a lot would go to so much effort to penetrate a woman's indifference. Surrounded by the packages of food, Amy suddenly broke into laughter. It was time to wave the white flag and admit that Max had won.

"Thank you for everything. It was wonderful. We'll be using you again." The words echoed repeatedly as Thor's executives filed out late that afternoon.

Amy shook hands and smiled as she stood in the foyer, bidding goodbye to the participants and telling each how much she enjoyed serving as hostess, feeling the fraud as she uttered the inanities. It had been a traumatic two days at best.

Max wasn't one of those departing and when Amy returned to the kitchen, he was there, leaning against the counter and chatting with Stephanie.

"He's all yours," Stephanie said, taking off her apron and handing it to Amy. "See you in the morning." She was out the door.

"I'm all yours," Max echoed.

"Seems that way." She hung Stephanie's apron on the peg, waiting to see what he'd do next.

"You've had a long day. Why don't I take you out to dinner?"

Amy eyed him skeptically. "What makes you think I'd consider going anywhere with you after the way you've picked on me?"

Showing no contrition, Max replied, "That's your fault for ignoring me. I only did what was necessary to get noticed. So now you can even the score at dinner. I'll be a sitting duck for you all through the meal. Come on, join me. Any place you say."

The twinge of pleasure that rippled through her couldn't be denied. While she now recognized Max's heckling for what it was, his confession helped eradicate any remaining hostility.

"You showed off like a schoolboy making faces at the teacher."

"I wasn't feeling at all like a little boy," he drawled provocatively.

"I could hardly do my job for trying to keep ahead of your pranks. It was diabolical of you to get so much pleasure out of them."

"Guilty as charged." He hung his head, rolling those bewitching eyes up to meet hers. "If you'll forgive me and accept my invitation, I promise I'll reform and be good," he said.

"Then you're admitting you've been *bad*."

Max smiled, the sort of smile that always tore down Amy's defenses. She remembered a remark once made about actor Warren Beatty and thought how appropriate it was to Max. "If he wants you to like him, there's no way not to like him."

But she wasn't going to cave in before giving Max one last dose of his own medicine. "I'm too tired for dinner tonight. Maybe another time when I'm in the mood."

"You sure know how to pander to a guy's ego."

"Your ego doesn't need pandering—it's sufficiently inflated without any input from me. Go away, Max." She made a swatting motion, as though shooshing a pesky fly.

Max grabbed the hand and kissed it. "No more. Fess up, Amy, you wouldn't let me get to the front door before running after me. Now be a good girl and get your purse."

She did as instructed.

Amy watched Max as he drove. Dark hairs lightly sprinkled the fingers that gripped the wheel. He really was an exceptional man. Not just inordinately handsome and a whiz at business, but genuinely nice, too—usually, anyway. Everyone who dealt with Max appeared to like him, all of her workers included.

She wished there were some way to magically banish her concerns. No matter how much chemistry existed between them, reality couldn't be avoided—their differences in background and social status, the fact their acquaintance could be numbered in weeks rather than months or years, the possibility she was a rebound romance for Max.

Amy adjusted the radio to a classical station and leaned her head against the leather headrest. The soothing music served to get her mind off negative thoughts. By the time they reached the restaurant, she'd convinced herself to postpone her worries and seize the moment.

The meal was tasty, the conversation easy and flowing, as both of them began to relax under the soft lights and casual atmosphere. After dinner Max invited her to his condominium.

Amy agreed without hesitation. Curiosity had overcome any remaining caution. Practically all their time together had been spent in her home. Even on their sporadic dates, they'd never gone to his place. Now she felt a need to.

Pulling up to the guarded garage gate of a high rise, Max was waved through by the attendant. He parked in the basement level and they took the elevator to the penthouse. Amy began second-guessing herself, wondering if she should be here. This was dangerous ground, but there was no excuse for changing her mind. None that Max would accept.

Would he have taken her home to Torrence Place if she'd asked? It didn't really matter because Amy didn't want to go there—not yet. While the outside of the luxurious building Max lived in was pretty much what she'd expected, she wanted to see his personal environment, the things he chose to surround himself with.

His home, which encompassed an entire floor, was spacious and airy with expanses of glass, oversize chairs and sofas, soft rugs, lush plants and a mixture of eye-catching oils and watercolors. Modern and comfortable, it spoke of a decorator's touch, yet complemented the man who resided there.

At his urging, Amy sat on one of the two plump sofas. When he sat next to her, she involuntarily stiffened.

"Why are you so afraid? I don't bite, you know. Well, I do nibble a little." He tilted toward her, playfully clicking his teeth together.

"I'm not afraid." She couldn't let his taunt stand, regardless of its merit.

"There you go, fibbing again. Yep," he said, "I do believe that nose is getting longer." He traced a thumb across her bottom lip, effectively silencing any reply. "I've had my quota of ribbing you today though, so I won't challenge you further...not tonight, anyway." He stole a kiss, a mere brush against her mouth, yet ardent enough to make Amy crave more. Temptation. That was Max Evans.

"Why did you bring me here?" she said.

"Why did you come?"

"I asked first."

He propped his hands on his knees as though composing an answer. Eventually he straightened, gazing directly into her eyes as he responded, "Because I want to start all over once again, to—"

That steadfast gaze caused Amy's heart to catch in her throat. "The harassment you've dished out the past two days was the action of a man who wants to start over? You've behaved like a...a..."

"Jerk? Heel? Horse's behind?"

"Worse than that."

He massaged his temples as if trying to conjure up something worse. "Arrogant, grind-'em-under-my-shoe corporate mogul? Spoiled, insensitive, know-it-all male chauvinist pig?"

Amy caught his grin and couldn't keep from giggling. "General all-purpose scoundrel—"

"How can I redeem myself?" he interrupted. "Can I begin by telling you how much I love you?"

"Uh-huh."

"And add that you've made me positively crazy by holding me at arm's length?"

"Uh-huh."

"And also add that I'm going to be a wreck of a man if you put me off any more?"

"Uh-huh."

"Can't I have a bit more feedback than that?"

"Oh, Max. I'm crazy about you, too. Wanting you has been driving me off a cliff."

He gathered her into his arms. "Does this mean your resistance is weakening?"

"Definitely," Amy said, welcoming his embrace. She had no idea what tomorrow might bring, but tonight Max was holding her and that was enough.

During the next week, Max consumed Amy's thoughts. But for a change, these were mostly positive thoughts with fewer forays into doubt. The only negative was that she missed him terribly.

He'd flown to Berlin, negotiating a sale with a German firm. During his absence he'd called daily. Brief calls, unsatisfying calls. Amy wanted him in Houston.

She remembered Max's charge that she was afraid. For the most part, Amy *had* lived a life of prudence, risking security only when she took over Torrence Place and started "Arrangements by Amy." Despite the ups and downs, that venture had turned out even better than she'd anticipated. For the second time she was going to have to follow her dream, to dare to stake her future again, a future with Max.

"I hate this," she complained to Stephanie when Thursday's workday ended. "Arrangements by Amy" was holding corporate meetings all week. Five different companies, one-day sessions each. Four down, one to go.

"What?" Stephanie looked over at her.

"These business functions. This is not what I set out to do."

"But they've solved the financial woes."

"True," Amy reluctantly agreed. "I guess I shouldn't look a gift horse in the mouth."

At periods like this Amy wished she were more like Stephanie. Amy was the fretter, Stephanie the optimist—and if Stephanie's optimism was misplaced, she could roll with the punches. She didn't end up tied in knots over situations she had no control over.

Steph and Jay might eat casseroles more often than steak, but Stephanie loved her nursing assignments and adored her husband. She even took joy in all the mundane tasks with Amy's business. Right now Amy hated her life. And now that she was opening her mind to the possibility of Max as a husband, he hadn't even mentioned marriage again. For all she knew, he might *never* bring it up again. All her hopes and plans could go awry. Amy was tired and unhappy and lovesick.

It was nine-thirty when the telephone rang—Max. Although he didn't discuss love or marriage, mostly he said all the right things, talked like a man who missed her, told her he'd see her the next day. But when Amy put down the phone, she felt more alone than ever. The conversation had been too brief. She wanted to talk in depth about their relationship.

Three more hours. She was apprehensive about seeing Max again, but no matter how many obstacles Amy had erected for them as a couple, she had taken a note from Stephanie's book and was being optimistic, daring to imagine an existence with him by her side. She could almost feel her heart soar as the minutes rolled off the clock. No more presidents and vice presidents and secretaries and comptrollers. She had a whole weekend free— a weekend she hoped to spend entirely with Max.

Max had suggested a date tonight and she had accepted before he could get the details out of his mouth.

Stephanie had left for an early shift at the hospital and Amy was clearing away the dirty coffee cups and leftover papers in the solarium. The rest of the cleanup couldn't wait until tomorrow.

She toted a plastic trash bag with her, dumping refuse as she circled the room. She grabbed a stack of brochures and annual reports and tossed them in. Apparently, the material didn't matter or it wouldn't have been left. One of the annual reports missed the bag and fell to the floor, lying open. "Max Evans Enterprises" the inside cover sheet read.

Amy dropped the trash and picked up the report. After studying it for a few moments, she glanced at her watch, then rushed to her office. It was just after four, probably not too late to get the information she needed.

Max called from Houston Intercontinental saying his plane was delayed and suggesting she meet him at his condo. The setting was incidental. Any place would suffice for the showdown Amy had in mind. Max might be plotting to lure her into his private domain for seduction, but Amy's thoughts ran more to homicide.

"How could you do this?" she hissed as Max opened the front door, shoving him away when he tried to take her into his arms.

"That's a hell of a greeting. What am I supposed to have done now?" he growled, reacting in kind to her furor.

"You didn't have any faith I could make it on my own, so you played fairy godfather." She waved the annual report in his face. "I thought I was doing so well, but you owned every damn one of those businesses coming into my place."

"Not every one." He went behind the bar and mixed himself a Scotch and soda. "I don't have a single share of stock in Computers Plus."

"But they came to Torrence Place because of you, because you recommended us. They just naturally assumed 'Arrangements by Amy' was the next best thing to microwave popcorn if the almighty Max Evans was referring them."

"So I intervened a little. Big deal. What difference does it make?"

Amy threw a hand in the air. *How could he be so dim-witted?* "All along I've turned down your offers of help. But you never got it, did you? I needed to climb out of my predicament on my own."

"I caused the predicament in the first place. I fix what I break."

"You used your influence to create business for me."

"So? It worked, didn't it? Can you honestly say you'd have survived without my help?"

"Believe me, I could survive without you!"

"No doubt. But would 'Arrangements by Amy' have made it?"

It would have been oh so gratifying to shout yes, but Amy knew her business would have sunk like the *Titanic* if he hadn't intervened. "Possibly not. But if I did make it, I'd have had the satisfaction of pulling myself up, not having someone rescue me."

"Is that so important to you?"

"Haven't you been listening to me? Yes, it's important."

"Then you don't belong in the business arena. Being successful means accepting help whenever and wherever it comes your way. As long as it's moral and legal, you take it. And it doesn't diminish your capabilities one iota."

"So what do you want—my eternal gratitude?"

"No, I just want you to behave like a sensible businesswoman, not a hysterical female."

"If you cared about me at all, you'd recognize why I feel so hurt. You'd—"

"*Care* about you? I've done every damn thing in the book to prove to you I care. Your problem is that you wouldn't recognize the truth if it were painted on a billboard in your front yard. I've said it before and I'll say it again. You're a fraud.

"You set yourself up as this big proponent of love, but Amy Holt doesn't really know what she's talking about. Love isn't all violins and candy. It's not a big show, a frothy confection of a wedding. It's everyday commitment, being there when you're needed, trying to help a person out if it's within your power to do so."

"Never having to say you're sorry when you're wrong?" His big speech sounded good, *too* good.

"No. It's being *able* to say you're sorry whenever you've fouled up. And being able to accept an apology when one is owed you."

"So are you apologizing?"

"For sending you business, no. For calling you a fraud, no. I stand by what I said. Take it or leave it."

"I see. I'm sure I sound terribly ungrateful, but I think I'll leave it. By the way, I despise training and business seminars. I never realized how much." When Max didn't respond, she added, "Maybe it's best that I go." She wanted him to argue with her, to wrap her in his arms, but he merely reached for her purse and handed it to her.

"Maybe it is," he said.

Amy meekly accepted the handbag and left, fighting tears. She got into her car and drove a few blocks, holding the steering wheel with one hand and wiping away the now-flowing tears with the other. When she noticed a coffee bar, she stopped. She could use a cup of solace right now, but coffee would be the next best thing. She needed a haven to regain her composure, to figure out just what had occurred at Max's.

Max was mistaken about her. She didn't think love was some fantasy. She knew it was give-and-take and— Had she done any giving? Not really. And she hadn't even been very good at taking.

So her pride was hurt to discover she hadn't saved her company single-handedly. Was pride so important, more important than love? Max may not have been the traditional knight on a white horse, but he had rescued her and she'd reacted like a woman betrayed. Although she disliked the business seminars, they had kept her afloat so that she could get back to what she loved best—weddings. Max would probably accuse her of never being satisfied. And he'd be right. How could she have been such an idiot?

A half hour later she was parked at the security gate of Max's condominium. "I'm sorry, ma'am, but Mr. Evans has gone out," the attendant advised. "Is there a message?"

"No...no message...good night."

When she returned to Torrence Place, Max was there, gently rocking on the swing. A gush of relief coursed through her whole body. "Oh, thank goodness," she said aloud, racing up the steps to meet him. Amy didn't know what to expect, but felt encouraged by the bouquets of flowers surrounding him—strictly last-minute supermarket purchases, but so many that several toppled off the swing when he rose.

"I was about to give up," he said.

"I went back to see you, but..."

"I'd already started after you." They stood apart, as though neither knew what to do or say, then Max took control. "I've obviously done a poor job of showing you how much I love you."

"No, oh, no," she protested. "I've been wearing blinders. Maybe you could show me again."

"And you'll believe it now?"

"I think I'm finally ready to."

"I was such a dunce, rushing you like some high schooler with raging hormones. No wonder you were wary. I should have been less impatient, more understanding. As you may have guessed, darling, I'm too used to getting what I want when I want it. My eagerness almost cost me what I hold most dear. I even pushed you into work you didn't like to salve my conscience and to hurry things along."

"We've both been fools. Everything happened too suddenly for me and I drew away like some threatened maiden."

"There's no reason for you to ever be threatened by me. Amy, you once said you wanted a man who couldn't bear waking up in the morning without you by his side. Well, dearest, I've developed a chronic case of insomnia. I don't want to fall asleep because you won't be there when I wake up and it's tearing me in pieces. I love you, Amy. Tell me what to do, how to say it better, because frankly, I'm at a loss."

From day one, Max was in charge, always had the answers, yet now he seemed vulnerable...just as she was. He'd said all she wanted, done all she wanted, now it was her turn. "I love you, too, Max. Desperately." She'd plunged in this far, why not go the course? "Is that marriage offer still open?"

He smiled. "Las Vegas? Tonight? Tomorrow?"

"Anywhere. Anytime. The sooner the better."

CHAPTER TWELVE

MAX gave her two hours to pack. As the reality began to sink in, Amy's inclination was to hyperventilate. She wasn't bemoaning her decision to marry, but she was torn as to her next course of action.

Should she call her parents? As an only child, she'd been close to them, accustomed to sharing pertinent tidbits about her life with them. Since she hadn't even mentioned Max, what would they think if she announced she was eloping? Would they be horrified, disappointed? There was no way to gauge their response and no way she could adequately explain by telephone. Perhaps she and Max could stop over in Dallas on the trip home. News like this should be delivered in person.

Then there was Stephanie. She would understand—be thrilled. Amy's only regret was that Steph was on duty with a patient instead of at home sharing in the euphoria. The happy news had to be related in a brief note. She could just hear Steph's squeals of joy when she read that note and learned Amy was going to be Mrs. Max Evans.

The thought brought a smile to her lips and helped Amy recover her composure. *No need to behave like a ninny.* She had no doubts about her feelings—or Max's. Amy Holt Evans. It sounded wonderful. Amy grabbed a suitcase from the closet and began assembling a makeshift trousseau.

Las Vegas could be laid-back or formal, so she'd take slacks and tops...her heather green chiffon cocktail dress... what else? Shoes, hose, underwear were tossed into the bag. She had no idea how long Max planned for them to stay, but if necessary she'd buy additional clothes.

She'd changed into a denim jumpsuit and packed her makeup when she remembered her most important item and rushed to the Bride's Room. This might be a spur-of-the-moment elopement, but she intended to look the part of a proper bride and the just-purchased antique wedding gown would ensure that she did.

Amy had never visited Las Vegas before, but all her expectations were fully met. The Vegas Strip lined with majestic hotels and lit by megawatts of neon was a tribute to excess, but with it came an aura of liveliness, a contagious excitement that captured her fancy.

She and Max had settled into luxurious suites at Caesar's Palace having decided to delay the actual ceremony until the next evening while Amy shopped for a veil and Max put the final touches on their arrangements. He had been unduly secretive. "You get to plan weddings all the time," he said. "Now it's my turn. And I want to do it by myself."

Max chose not one of the well-known chapels, but a small traditional church in a residential area. He had kept the destination a mystery until Amy's arrival. It was a beautiful church, but even more beautiful was the sight of her parents, standing on the sidewalk as the limousine drove up. Her father opened the car door and assisted her out. "How...?" She was too astonished to complete the question.

"We'll go over that later," her father assured her, as both parents gave her hugs and kisses. "But in the meantime, your groom is waiting."

Over the years Amy had envisioned many scenarios for her own wedding...the old family church in Houston, one of the yacht clubs on Galveston Bay—or more exotically, a Caribbean beach or the wine country of France...but none of those places could compare with the rites Max had arranged. His parents and sisters, brothers-in-law and their children were there. As were Jenna, Stephanie and Jay. Stephanie, her matron of honor, exactly as Amy had wanted. Aaron West was standing up for Max.

"No second thoughts?" Stephanie asked, handing Amy an elaborate bouquet of white roses and baby's breath.

"None whatsoever...absolutely none," Amy answered as she took her father's arm and the organ began playing "Jesu, Joy of Man's Desiring." How had Max known her favorite music? Steph, no doubt. Again, another of Amy's wedding dreams fulfilled. But the best dream, the only one of real importance, was Max—the man at the end of that aisle.

Following the ceremony, everyone proceeded to a reception at a suite in the hotel. On the drive there, Max told Amy about calling her father to ask for his blessing. Described how, with input from her mother and Stephanie, he'd managed to organize the wedding in less than twenty-four hours. "Jenna helped, too. She said she owed you after putting you on the spot with her own wedding."

"It was perfect. You're perfect." Amy grasped the lapels of Max's tuxedo and pulled him to her for a kiss.

"I wanted to make all your wedding fantasies come true, to prove to you how deeply, how completely, I've fallen in love."

"So you've become a convert," Amy teased.

"Unequivocally. I'll be boring people silly bragging about what an extraordinary wife I have ... what terrific children."

"We haven't talked about having a family." The realization shocked her. Max had indicated a desire for children when discussing his proposal to Robin, but that was as far as the subject had gone. "There are so many things we don't know about each other."

"We have a lifetime to discover them. Do you want a baby?"

"More than one."

"Four or five then?"

She laughed. "Not quite that many. Let's go for one to begin with."

Max's eyes burned with desire. "We'll start on it as soon as I can push everyone out the door."

Amy nestled into his embrace, happy, content. "Even in my fantasies, I didn't know love could be like this."

"Me neither. Until you came along, I'd convinced myself I'd never feel this way about anyone," he said. "Then we met and it was as though a void I wasn't aware of had been filled. I'll cherish you all of my days, Mrs. Evans." He lifted her face to his and there was no more conversation for the rest of the trip to the reception.

Guests were greeted, the toasts completed and the traditional cake cutting over when Amy heard a voice much resembling "The King's" crooning "Love Me Tender." A spotlight announced the appearance of an Elvis Presley impersonator who was soon joined by a quartet of clones, all dressed in white-spangled bodysuits, necks draped with flowing red scarfs. "I couldn't let you be disappointed with your Las Vegas wedding," Max said, nodding toward the group of look-alikes. "And I knew you wouldn't think it complete without the Elvis touch."

Amy gazed up at him. "It's been everything I hoped for."

"Not too gaudy?" Max asked, easing her into an embrace.

She laughed. "This is Las Vegas. There's no such thing as too gaudy. It would have been fitting even if it'd taken place in front of one of the roulette tables in the middle of the casino—"

"I didn't want you to feel you were taking any gambles," Max interrupted.

"No gamble," Amy answered. "After all, we have a sure thing. We have love."

"Yes," he echoed. "Forever and always."

Harlequin Romance®

brings you

SIMPLY THE BEST

*Authors you'll treasure,
books you'll want to keep!*

Harlequin Romance just keeps getting better and better...and we're delighted to welcome you to our **Simply the Best** showcase for 1997, highlighting a special author each month!

These are stories we know you'll love reading—again and again! Because they are, quite simply, the best...

Don't miss these unforgettable romances coming to you in May, June and July.

> **May—GEORGIA AND THE TYCOON (#3455)**
> **by Margaret Way**
> **June—WITH HIS RING (#3459)**
> **by Jessica Steele**
> **July—BREAKFAST IN BED (#3465)**
> **by Ruth Jean Dale**

Available wherever Harlequin books are sold.

Free Gift Offer

With a Free Gift proof-of-purchase
from any Harlequin® book, you can receive
a beautiful cubic zirconia pendant.

This stunning marquise-shaped stone is a genuine cubic
zirconia—accented by an 18" gold tone necklace.
(Approximate retail value $19.95)

Send for yours today...
compliments of ◈HARLEQUIN®

To receive your free gift, a cubic zirconia pendant, send us one original proof-of-purchase, photocopies not accepted, from the back of any Harlequin Romance®, Harlequin Presents®, Harlequin Temptation®, Harlequin Superromance®, Harlequin Intrigue®, Harlequin American Romance®, or Harlequin Historicals® title available in February, March or April at your favorite retail outlet, together with the Free Gift Certificate, plus a check or money order for $1.65 U.S./$2.15 CAN. (do not send cash) to cover postage and handling, payable to Harlequin Free Gift Offer. We will send you the specified gift. Allow 6 to 8 weeks for delivery. Offer good until April 30, 1997, or while quantities last. Offer valid in the U.S. and Canada only.

Free Gift Certificate

Name: _____

Address: _____

City: _____ State/Province: _____ Zip/Postal Code: _____

Mail this certificate, one proof-of-purchase and a check or money order for postage and handling to: HARLEQUIN FREE GIFT OFFER 1997. In the U.S.: 3010 Walden Avenue, P.O. Box 9071, Buffalo NY 14269-9057. In Canada: P.O. Box 604, Fort Erie, Ontario L2Z 5X3.

FREE GIFT OFFER   084-KEZ

ONE PROOF-OF-PURCHASE

To collect your fabulous FREE GIFT, a cubic zirconia pendant, you must include this original proof-of-purchase for each gift with the properly completed Free Gift Certificate.

084-KEZ

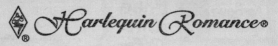

Harlequin Romance®

is proud to announce the latest arrivals
in our bouncing baby series

Each month in 1997 we'll be bringing you your very
own bundle of joy—a cute, delightful romance by
one of your favorite authors. Our heroes and heroines
are about to discover that two's company and three
(or four...or five) is a family!

Find out about the true labor of love...

Don't miss these charming stories
of parenthood, and how to survive it,
coming in May, June and July.

**May—THE SECRET BABY (#3457)
by Day Leclaire
June—FOR BABY'S SAKE (#3461)
by Val Daniels
July—BABY, YOU'RE MINE! (#3463)
by Leigh Michaels**

Available wherever Harlequin books are sold.

Happy Birthday to

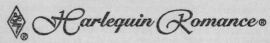 *Harlequin Romance*®

With the purchase of three Harlequin Romance books, you can send in for a **FREE** hardbound collector's edition and automatically enter Harlequin Romance's 40th Anniversary Sweepstakes.

FREE COLLECTOR'S EDITION BOOK

On the official entry form/proof-of-purchase coupon below, fill in your name, address and zip or postal code, and send it, plus $1.99 U.S./$2.99 CAN. for postage and handling (check or money order—please do not send cash), payable to Harlequin Books, to: In the U.S.: 3010 Walden Avenue, P.O. Box 9071, Buffalo, N.Y. 14269-9071; In Canada: P.O. Box 622, Fort Erie, Ontario L2A 5X3. Please allow 4-6 weeks for delivery. Order your **FREE** Collector's Edition now; quantities are limited. Offer for the free hardbound book expires December 31,1997. Entries for the Specially Autographed 40th Anniversary Collector's Edition draw will be accepted only until July 31, 1997.

WIN A SPECIALLY AUTOGRAPHED COLLECTOR'S EDITION BOOK

To enter Harlequin Romance's 40th Anniversary Sweepstakes only, hand print on a 3" x 5" card the words "Harlequin Romance's 40th Anniversary Sweepstakes," your name and address and mail to: "40th Anniversary Harlequin Romance Sweepstakes"—in the U.S., 3010 Walden Avenue, P.O. Box 9076, Buffalo, N.Y. 14269-9076; in Canada, P.O. Box 637, Fort Erie, Ontario L2A 5X3. No purchase or obligation necessary to enter. Limit: one entry per envelope. Entries must be sent via first-class mail and be received no later than July 31, 1997. See back-page ad for complete sweepstakes rules.

Happy Birthday, Harlequin Romance!

Official Entry Form/Proof of Purchase

"Please send me my **FREE**
40th Anniversary Collector's Edition book and enter me in
Harlequin Romance's 40th Anniversary Sweepstakes."

Name: _____

Address: _____

City: _____

State/Prov.: _____ Zip/Postal Code: _____

089-KEP

089-KEP